WICHITA
U.S. MARSHALL

WICHITA
U.S. MARSHALL

Jedediah Ravine

Studio of Books LLC
5900 Balcones Drive Suite 100
Austin, Texas 78731
www.studioofbooks.org
Hotline: (254) 800-1183

Ordering Information:
Special discounts are available on quantity purchases by corporations, associations, and others. For details, contact the publisher at the address above.

Printed in the United States of America.

ISBN-13: Softcover   978-1-964928-36-4
          Hardcover   978-1-964928-37-1
          eBook   978-1-964928-38-8

Library of Congress Control Number: 2025907992

Contents

PREFACE

When I was a kid, I loved getting up on Saturday morning to watch the Lone Ranger.

I'll never forget "HI O SILVER AWAY"

As I grew up, I remember watching John Wayne, Gene Autry, Rocky Lane and the movies they made where the good guys always win. How Roy Rogers never killed anybody and simply shot the gun out of the villain's hands.

Good was good, bad was bad, and when something was inbetween, good always won out in the end.

Gunsmoke was one of the best about that, and I still watch it to this day. Man I sure miss those days. As I recall, it was in the late sixties when western movies started to change, not more violent necessarily, for violence was always a part of the old west both in reality and in stories especially in the 1880's. However, the stories became more complicated, at least for me. Moreover, boundaries between good and evil became blurry. The good was just the "best of the bad" it seemed. Foul language and explicit scenes of sex and graphic violence were the feature. They called it REVISIONIST.

For the most part, they lost life's lessons where heroes were both strong and kind. They were honorable defenders of the common folk, especially the week and the vulnerable. Keeping these things in mind, I wrote my story – a story of the real and difficult struggles of good men.

These were men of courage and commitment such as Rangers, Sheriffs, and U.S. Marshalls. This story is told without useless profanity and over emphasis on the graphic nature of evil deeds by villains.

A story even youngsters can listen to and learn something about the unintended consequences of "acting on" even righteous indignation. There are lessons about the power of friendship and love.

That was my hope.

It may sound old fashion, it may sound out of the mainstream of modern 'revisionist' tales of the old West, but I invite you to read or listen to my story. In this fully produced Audio Book "Wichita U S Marshall".

Close your eyes sit back hear the excitement!

Hear the heart and soul of a tale for everyone, young and old.

Follow the life of Wichita U S Marshall and his struggles external and Internal.

Like one of your favorite old movies you'll listen again and again.

CHAPTER 1

The Beginning and a Bad Day in Durango

In ancient history, when the sons of God rebelled both in heaven and earth, evil and violence became the order of things. The Creator put in place a mandate, a task to duly authorized authorities to deal with evil deeds and to curb anarchy.

In the time and place known as the Wild West, this task fell upon the good and the brave men such as the town sheriffs, rangers, and U.S. Marshals. That task became the code of the lawman. It was recorded in God's own book, for there it says,

"For they stand placed by God for your good. But if you do bad, be in fear for they bare the sword as God's minister, as an avenger against evil deeds."

Well, they called it the Wild West. It was a new land filled with opportunities for adventurous men and women. There was land to be had and fortunes to be made in cattle, in building towns, railroads, and such. And besides that, there was gold, especially in the Rocky Mountains, and with all that, came all sorts of men -- good and bad. At times it seemed that the bad outnumbered the good, and the good were forced to deal with them often in brutal and harsh ways. For where there's gold, there's greed. For where there's greed, there's killing and stealing, and all kinds of villainous things in between.

Well, it was in such times that the man in my story lived. This is the story of Wichita, U.S. Marshal.

Now I was sipping on sweet tea like I did most every day around that time, just watching people as they went about their day, and saying my howdys to folks that walked by within hearing distance. That was part of my job being the local lawman in those days.

Nothing really special about that day, it was like most clear spring days in the Rocky Mountains. Except for this young man I'd never seen before. Riding into town, sitting tall in the saddle so to speak – meaning he looked proud and confident but he had a friendly manner and he had a great big smile. I also noticed one other thing that kinda struck me, not odd but just curious. A sidearm, it was a long-barreled .44. I knew weapons, and I hadn't seen one of these in a while. Well, little did I know that that long-barreled .44 would become well known in these parts for years to come.

Well as I was pondering this, suddenly a young strong voice said,

"Morning Marshal. Beautiful day, isn't it?

Sure is, son. Who might you be." "I'm Wichita."

"Well, where are you from, son?"

"Oh, lots of places."

"Are you just passing through?"

"No, Marshal. I am here to see a girl. The prettiest girl in town."

"Well, that explains it " I thought to myself, "Only a pretty girl could put a smile on a cowboy like this one had."

"What might be this little gal's name be?"

"Her name? Her name is springtime in the Rocky's. Fresh caught trout simmered over a fire. The clearest star-filled sky you've ever seen. The sight of a clear, cool spring to a man dying of thirst. But most folks just call her Annie."

"Annie Wakefield?"

"Do you know her, Marshal?"

"Well, I sure do. You must be the young man Annie's father told me about."

Well, right in the middle of my talking, Annie comes running and hollering,

"Oh, Wichita you're here."

And in the blink of an eye, they're embracing each other and kissing.

Right in front of the whole town.

Now apparently, these two had met when Annie's father sent her to Denver for some kind of schooling. And I have to admit when she got back, she had a look and a way about her I never thought any school or learning could make if you get my meaning and apparently, I was right.

Well, a short time later, I found myself acting as justice of the peace. Which was another part of my job, and so I married Wichita and Annie. Now I seldom ever seen Wichita without a smile. And about a year later, that smile turned into an ear-to-ear grin, for Annie had given birth to a healthy, blue-eyed baby boy.

Well, 10 years passed, and Wichita became a friend to everyone in town. Him, Annie, little Luke. He not only befriended everyone, but he proved himself to be a protector of the town as well. For instance, the first time I'd ever seen him use that long-barreled .44, and this was what happened.

One afternoon two strangers rode into town, and it was plain to see that they'd been riding long, and hard. Their mounts were lathered pretty good, and when they stepped off their horses, there was as much dust on them as there was on the trail that they came in on.

I was in the saloon when they walked in. After they were there for a bit. I noticed their mannerism was fidgety and unsettled. Now I was sitting near the window next to the main street. But them two cowboys, they didn't notice me. At least they hadn't noticed my badge. Just as I was about to approach them two and inquire who they were and what they were doing in my town. I heard Annie saying to Wichita,

"Now don't be in there too long, you hear? Or there will be heck to pay."

And then Wichita walked through the door. Well, he noticed me, and he called out,

"Hey Marshal, how you doing?"

Them two cowboys instantly knocked over the tables they were sitting at and drew down on them shooters. I went for mine but quick as thought, Wichita had drawn that .44 and fired twice. Them two strangers lay dead on the saloon floor.

Now, these villains had robbed a train just a few miles outside of Silverton and figured that they'd gotten away but they were wrong.

Now that was the first time Wichita had come to my aid when facing dangerous men. But it was not the last, that was for sure and for certain.

So, when it came time for me to step aside and take life easier for a change, there was little doubt and absolutely no dispute whom the town folk would want for the next sheriff.

Fact was , Wichita was reluctant at first but not because of some phony humility. He knew he was the most qualified in town. Rather, he was reluctant because of Annie and little Luke. But because he was how he was and knowing the need and having a sense of duty, Wichita took the job. Eventually, he was appointed the United States Marshal, given the authority of the entire state of Colorado. Things went well for several years and Durango, for the most part, stayed a peaceful town. That was until the morning of July 5, 1888. That's a day I'll never forget.

Now I had been used to getting up early every morning most of my life and that morning wasn't no different. Even though it was quite the celebration the night before, being it was Independence Day. And oh, what a celebration it was. People came from all over to see fireworks, and to eat, and drink, and even dance with purdy girls. I'd seen folks I hadn't seen all year, even folks I'd never seen before, cowboys and the like.

Well, I was staying in the room behind the jailhouse them days. Being I was acting as a part-time deputy. I guess I couldn't get away completely from the law game, as it were. I didn't do much, I just kept the place clean, did some paperwork, and helped out whenever Wichita was out of town, which that day, he happened to be.

I had just stepped outside when I saw skip barrel cleaning the streets. Boy, they were a mess. Besides him and me, there wasn't much movement in town. I was on my second pot of coffee and ol' skip barrel had just about got the streets cleaned up when I noticed Annie and little Luke stepping into the general store to get some supplies, I reckon.

Just then I heard several gunshots. Now you see the bank of Durango was situated just on the backside of that general store and it dawned on me that that is where the commotion was coming from. Just as I stood up to grab a rifle and head in that direction. The sound of six horses running hard filled the morning air. The next sound I heard was even more terrifying. Annie and Luke were just coming out of the general store at the same time that the outlaws came around the corner. I heard Annie call out,

"Luke, oh my God, Luke!" And then I heard Luke call out, "Mom!"

Annie screamed, and then there was just the sound of horses and riders leaving town. Well, when the dust cleared, both Annie and Luke's bodies lay in the street, trampled, torn, and broken.

Now later that day, around 6:30 in the evening, when the sun was still giving off some light behind the mountains west of the Durango. The town had somewhat settled down to the bad things that had happened that day. Besides Annie and Luke, these villains had shot and killed little Sally Wilson. She was the bank owner's daughter. She just stopped by to tell her daddy that she was on her way to school and she loved him. They shot her right through the throat; besides that, the bank manager, they shot him twice. He'll live but he ain't never gonna walk again. Now we'd talked about getting a posse together, but most just wanted to wait for the Marshal. Besides, by the time townsfolk had gotten over the shock of that day, no one knew where to start. The outlaws they had hours ahead of us and they were riding hard.

Annie's father, he came by the office and sat in down the chair. Just across from the Marshal's desk. He just sat there for a few seconds. Then he looked up and said,

"Have you heard anything from the marshal?"

"No William, I haven't." and then he broke down and he cried.

Right then, I heard a faint voice from the distance saying "It's Wichita. The Marshal is back." William and I had run out of door, and at the edge of the town, we could see Wichita riding slowly into town. Sitting tall like usual, looking forward to getting home to Annie and little Luke. Well, I wanted to be the one to tell him what had happened because I knew he would take it hard. But before I could get to him, a couple of young boys ran up to the Marshal and told him about his wife and his son.

I was watching from the jail porch and I could see a change in his whole demeanor, he slapped that mount came riding hard towards the jailhouse. When he got to me, dust was a flying and the Marshal dismounted right in the middle of it when I could finally see his face clear, it was a look that I had never seen before. His eyes were tight and squinty, his jaw was clinched and hard. He just stared at me for a second or two and then he said, "where are they? Annie and Luke."

"Follow me." And I took him to the undertaker's place. Well, I stayed outside, and he went in alone. William and I, we waited outside the undertaker's place for, I don't know, maybe an hour. And then I decide to go back to the jail and wait for the Marshal there. William went back home to try and find peace in his own way. Now William was a god-fearing man, and he would leave things in His and the law's hands as he put it.

Well, it was dark by now, and the streets were unusually quiet. Even the saloon was missing the normal sound of piano playing and the sounds of cowboys and saloon girls and such. Laughing and carrying on. But then I heard footsteps walking on the boardwalk just outside the jail. So, I stepped outside.

"Marshal, I'm so sorry. It happened so fast. I felt so helpless. I loved Annie and Luke, and I'd given my life to save them if I could"

Wichita with his hand on the saddle and his head bowed down. He turned his head and raised his eyes slightly. "I know that, Jed. Don't you know, I know that. You tell me, what direction did they take."

"They headed west, riding hard." "How many?"

"There were six."

"Listen, I know you ain't up to this. But I need you to take care of things around here for a while. I don't know how long it is going to take. But Im

I'm gonna find E'm , I'm gonna find E'm all, no matter where they are."

"Listen Marshal, you know by morning we could have fifty men ready to ride. There ain't a man in this town that won't ride with you."

"I'll do this alone. Don't you follow me, I am leaving tonight."

Now up to then with exception of dealing with wild cowboys from time to time. No one really knew much about Marshal's ability with guns and other things. He never talked much about his past, no one really knew where he was from. But through the years I came to know a little about his life before Annie.

I know he lived back East for a while and when about 14 years of age, he left his folks and found his way out West. He worked as a cow hand for a while and found that life, like many do, not to be his liking. He eventually ended up working as a scout for the Texas rangers. Tracking Indians, Mexican bandits, as such. And at the young age of 18 years, he was already considered one of the best trackers and one of the deadliest marksmen amongst the Texas Rangers. Fact is that about 20 years old, he was hired as a detective by the Pinkerton Detectives to seek out desperate men in and around Denver, Colorado. Which is where he met Annie for the first time. Whoever these bad men were that had robbed and killed in Durango that day. This was no ordinary man on their trail and it was plain to see that retribution and the fast hand of the law would eventually catch up to them.

Now the rest of the story, I am going to tell you from the things that I heard. Because I did just as the Marshal asked me, I didn't follow him. This is a tale of a man driven by the need and the duty to hand out justice on behalf of those whose lives were taken so tragically and with absolutely no remorse. Know this, to every man, those that Wichita hunted down were men who gave no thought to killing, to robbing, or hurting innocent folks. These weren't just outlaws; these were men who needed to be stopped. For they would kill again and this duly appointed lawman would fulfill that need.

CHAPTER 2

The Trail to Silverton and Then To Pagosa Springs

Now Wichita had been tracking these outlaws since first light. He was moving slow, looking for a sign so that he could stay on their trail. Now towards dusk, the trail took an unexpected turn. The gang of outlaws split up in three directions; straight west, more than likely towards Dolores – the railroad went through their regular. North, towards Silverton and East, maybe to the Springs… Pagosa Springs. A good place to soothe saddle sores after a long, hard ride.

Now the Marshal had a decision to make. The trail indicated that one went west, two headed north, and three headed east. Wichita decided head to Silverton which was a mining town. Full of all the things men like these would want – gambling, drinking, women, and such. It was about 25 miles to Silverton from where Wichita came to the split in the trail. That was 25 hard miles over and through rough mountain country.

Two days later, the Marshal could see the town of Silverton and was sure he would find at least 2 of the 6 men that he was determined to hand out justice to. It was almost dark, and the Marshal decided to wait till dark to come in town. He had no idea where he would find these outlaws, but he decided that the saloon would be a good place to start. So, he rides into town. He walks into saloon, sits at the table towards the back, and just watched and listened.

Now he had sat for several hours and was unable to identify anyone. "Maybe they moved on," he thought to himself. Anyway, he was tired and dirty, and he needed some rest. So, he decided to go to the boarding house and get some rest.

Well, after paying for the room. The desk clerk asked the Marshal, "sir, would you like a bath before you go to your room."

"A bath, that sounds good". So, he headed for the bathhouse. There he came upon a little old lady with towels standing next to a large pot of boiling water. She said to the Marshal, "you want the first bath, the second, or the third?"

"What's the difference?"

"The cleaner the water, the higher the price." "Well, alright, give me the first."

Now it'd been a while since Wichita took a bath. In fact, it was Annie that insisted that he'd take that bath. And as he laid there, overtaken by the steam and the hot water, and the smell of lilac and such. He could vision Annie laughing, and playing, and ending up in that tub with him. Holding and touching her.

Suddenly, two drunken cowboys fall right through the door, in the marshal's stall. With Whiskey on their breath and a bottle in their hand. Well, they excused themselves and returned to laughing, and carrying on into the tubs next to him.

Then one of the cowboys says something that catches the marshal's attention.

This is what he heard.

"I'm telling you Billy. Just one more job like that one in Durango and we can retire for good. Head on down to Mexico. Live as kings. Ain't no law can follow us down there."

"You're right, and if they do. We'll take care of 'em just like we did back in Ouray".

Instantly, Wichita's thought turned from the peacefulness of being in the arms of Annie, to the intense rage that he felt in his heart towards these murdering cowards just a few feet away. His first thought was to simply walk over and kill them in their tubs.

But they wouldn't know by whom or why they met this fate. Besides, the Marshal knew that the right thing to do would be to inform the local law what his intentions towards these men were and to make it perfectly clear that they were wanted dead or alive.

Now the Marshal wouldn't take any chances of losing these two. So, he waited outside the bathhouse till these two men came out still drunk and stumbling all over each other. Wichita watched as these outlaws went to their rooms. He then went to his own room and he fell asleep.

That night he dreamed of Annie and Luke and the life they had. Annie laughing and playing with little Luke and then looking up at Wichita and saying with her sweet smile, "I love you." Then that sweet smile turning into a face of complete terror and Annie screaming. Waking Wichita up in cold sweat.

Realizing that was now early the next morning. The Marshal rose, strapped on his colt, and walked into the local sheriff 's office and informed the sheriff that he was the U.S. Marshal from Durango. Sent here to capture, if possible, two of six bandits, wanted for robbery and murder. He handed the sheriff two John Doe warrants and told them he had identified these bandits the night before and he knew their whereabouts.

Well Wichita asked the Sherriff, "Do you wanna help?" "I guess I should."

"Then just stay out of my way."

And then he turned and he left. Now Wichita walked to the center of the main street. Just outside of the boarding house. He noticed both of them outlaws drinking coffee just inside the parlor. He could see them through the plate glass window. He kneeled over, not taking his eyes off of those two men for even a second. Tied his holster down with that long-barreled .44 and stood straight. Staring right at the cowboys until they saw him and then Billy noticed him.

"Clayton, do you see that?"

Indicating what by moving his eyes in the direction of the street. They knew they were being called out. And being curious and full of themselves, they stood up and walked out and stood before the man on the street. Billy then noticed the marshal's badge. Then he spoke up, "Marshal, you looking for us?"

"I'm looking for two cowards that robbed and murdered in my town.

If that be you, the answer's yes, I'm taking you boys in."

Without pause, the two men went for their shooters. Their hands had barely touched their pistol grips when the Marshal pulled his Colt, fired four shots. Striking both, center chest, and in the throat.

The Marshal hadn't for a second, forgotten little Sally Wilson. Well, for a moment he just stood there, took a deep breath and sighed just a little.

Someone said they thought that they heard him say, "four more Annie. Four more."

Now the town sheriff. He came running to the middle of the street. Then he walked over to the dead men and said, "I don't know who these men are. Never seen them before in these parts. You sure they are the ones?"

"I asked 'em. They answered when they pulled them shooters." And then he mounted up and he rode away.

Now Luke was just eight years old and he'd been asking his father for weeks if he could have a horse of his own. Annie had been reluctant to say yes knowing how dangerous them lame brain critters can be, as she used to put it. But Luke was a strong-spirited boy, even extra so for his age. Much like his father. After all, he struck out on his own at the young age of 14 years.

Now Wichita had just returned from a visit to one of the local miners and had purchased a fine young pony at the price of $50. Now he did this without Annie's knowledge or permission. Now, in most things, he always respected Annie's permission issues if you know what I mean. Anyway, Wichita knew that once Annie seen the look on Luke's face.

She couldn't stay mad for long. At least, he'd hope so. Now Luke was outside gathering water when his father came in the view. Luke looked once, squinted his eyes, stretched out his neck and then yelled, "Maa, Pa's home and he ain't alone."

Well, Annie wasn't within hearing distance because she was out back behind the barn doing some wash by the creek. Wichita came closer and Luke, as fast as his little legs would carry him, closed the gap between 'em until they met each other about one hundred feet from the house.

"Pa, you did it. You got me a horse, didn't you, pa? "Sure did, son. He's all yours."

Little Luke, overcome with excitement says, "Can I ride him, pa. Can I?"

Now Wichita had bought the horse at such a good price mainly cause it

weren't full broke yet, it was still pretty green and like little Luke, full of life and spirit. Reluctantly and looking around to see if Annie was watching, he said, "okay son, mount up."

Well that horse took to bucking and snorting like a whirlwind and little Luke was holding on for dear life. Then suddenly Luke went flying ten feet in the air and landed on his backside. Much, to everyone's surprise, right next to Annie. With a mixture of laughter and fear, Wichita ran over to check on Luke. Annie clearly angry hit Wichita on the arm in a gesture of disapproval. Being she stood about one foot shorter than he did and weighed about 95 pounds. That's all hitting ever did. It just meant, "I ain't happy."

Well, Annie and Wichita kneeled down and say together at the same time,

"Luke, are you okay?"

And Luke looked up and said, "was that some ride or what, pa?" And then all three started laughing out loud.

Wichita suddenly rose out of his bed roll, awakened by the sound of his horse rearing and acting spooked. At the same moment, in an instance, he pulls his Colt, trying to focus from dream sleep, to consciousness. Slowly focusing in on what spooked his horse. It was a female mountain lion perched on the large boulder just 15 or 20 feet away. Wichita keeps his Colt fixed and softly says . "Don't worry girl. I ain't gonna hurt ya."

He then notices two small cubs just behind her mama and Wichita says, "go on girl, take care of your family."

Now the sun was not quiet peaking over the eastern ridge but it was light enough that he decided to break camp and continue tracking these three outlaws that he was sure were heading east towards Pagosa Springs. He saddled his horse and as he was pulling the cinch on his saddle tight, the sun came brilliantly over the east ridge. Wichita stood perfectly still for a moment. Thinking about Annie, her bright smile, her sky blue eyes, her touch, her smell. The softness of her voice. All this that he'd never see again. Overwhelmed with a broken heart, Wichita screams Annie's name with all his might. At that moment, about three days ride away.

"Jake, did you hear that?" "Hear what?"

"I thought I heard someone call out. You know, like a name or something."

"You were dreaming and thanks for waking me up." "Where's Tom?" cares?"

"Ah, he must be relieving himself or something. Who knows. Who

About that time Tom Jenkins. a tall, heavy, older man with long hair and a mean disposition comes from around behind a large boulder and says, "saddle up, boys. We gotta get down the trail, we gotta ways to go to get to that bank. Besides, I wanna get to them hot tubs down there in the Pagosa Springs and ease my bones a bit."

Just then, Willy, the youngest of the three and the most easily spooked notices something in the trees just a head.

"Did you see that?"

"See what? What is it this time, boy?" He sees it again, "there, you see that?"

All three look in the direction Willy is pointing and sure enough, there is someone there. Whoever it is, appears to be small, and quickly high tails it out of there. The three bandits follow. Now just over ridge, the outlaws lose sight of the one they are chasing, but they spot a small cabin in the valley below.

Jake takes notice, "look, there's smoke down there in that chimney.

Someone must be there."

Tom says, "we need some supplies, coffee, some food and I need me a little fun. Let's see what we can find."

Just then a man and a woman come out of the cabin, the woman goes to the well and the man to the outhouse. Tom tells Willy and Jake, "work your down there and deal with that. I'll take care of the women."

Now these were bad, evil men – caring for nothing, but their own wants, needs, and pleasures. As for what happened next? Well that's all that needs to be said.

Now Wichita had been hard on the trail for two days. The men he was after were careless and sloppy when it came to covering their tracks. Now that meant that they were either stupid and that they just didn't care if anyone was following them or not. An attitude that they gave the Marshal a definite advantage or made them very dangerous.

If they thought they could come into Durango and rob and murder innocent folk. And escape with no one following them, that would make them easy to catch. If they just didn't care, and just waiting for someone to get close. Well, they would more than likely wait in ambush, and in the rocky mountains there were plenty of places to set up just such a plan. Still, the Marshal was determined to find these men and he would keep his mind clear and his senses keen.

About dusk, he had decided to set up camp for the night, rest his mount, and clear his head a little. The trail was clear and there was little or no sign of rain or snow and he was sure that the trail would be easy to pick up in the morning. Now a creek ran nearby and he decided to catch some trout and have a hot meal for a change. He fashioned himself a fishing line and went to catching several trout, his favorite. He had just set some in the fire and the smell was such as brought some peacefulness to his mind. Then he began to picture the first time he and Annie had trout together and a smile appeared on his face.

As husband and wife, Wichita and Annie had spent their very first night together. In a small cabin, he'd built. Not alone, mind you, but with Annie's help. They'd just finished the cabin and hadn't given much thought to supplies like food and such. So, early the next morning, Wichita heads to the creek and catches breakfast. You guessed it. Trout. While Annie slept, he cooks the fish over a fire in the cabin fireplace. Now, like most relationships, Wichita didn't yet know everything about Annie, but in time, he would learn. For one thing, Annie hated fish. I mean hated fish. But she loved Wichita. When she got out of bed that morning, she could smell those trout cooking. She peeked her head out the door and saw her husband setting the table, lighting candles and, just generally, being a real romantic fella. She didn't have the heart to tell him that she hated fish and had never eaten any trout. Now trout are small fish with some bones and you have to be careful when eating them. Well Annie had made up her mind to just eat the fish this one time, and later, let Wichita know that she hated fish.

"Good morning, dear."

"Good morning. Did you sleep well?" "I sure did."

Wichita gives her a kiss on the cheek and nervously sets her down to breakfast.

"I never made breakfast for anyone but myself before. I hope you like it."

"Looks good"

Well Annie bravely takes a bite of the trout and successfully swallows it down and manages to keep a smile on her face at the same time. Wichita, after seeing Annie was pleased, digs in and starts to eaten. Annie takes one more bite and her stomach starts to quiver and jerk inward and she feels a little sick, but takes one more tiny bite and bites on a bone. It sticks in top of her mouth and that's all she can take. She starts choking and tries to pull out the bone but the stomach won't hold it any longer. Wichita jumps out of his chair, comes to Annie's aid and she spews all over him.

Well they both fall on the floor, sliding around in lumpy liquid. Annie looks up at Wichita and says, "I'm so sorry."

Wichita smiles and softly says, "I love you," and they both burst out laughing. For just a brief moment, Wichita had slipped into a peace of mind, and he laughs out loud, shaking his head. Remembering how wonderfully silly they were that day. Suddenly, something breaks the mood. Wichita hears horses in the distance. He quickly covers his fire and dirt, making sure that no smoke rises. He goes to his horse and slowly and quietly begins to saddling. All along, looking in the direction of the sound of the horses that he hears in the distance.

He leads his horses into some thick trees and just waits. As the sounds get closer, it becomes clear it's more than just one rider and by the sound of the horses, it's likely these ain't cowboys. There was no sound of leather, nor the sound of metal bits. The footsteps of the horses were soft, indicating unshod ponies. As the riders came into view, it became clear they were indeed Indians. "But these were Arapahoe. What were they doing so far south," He thought to himself. This was Comanche country and besides, most Arapahoe were in Wyoming on the Shoshoni reservation. Now these were young bucks, painted for battle. He hadn't seen a war party in years and he decided it would be best to confront these young men now and find out their intent rather than have them catch him unaware on the trail later on.

So, he stepped out in plain sight. Well, Wichita spoke a little Arapahoe in his younger days as a scout and he found out that these young men were hunting six white men who had come up on a small village and murdered several families and burned the village to the ground. Now these boys were out hunting when it happened, and when they returned, they found their families dead, beaten, and worse. They informed the authorities but were told they were shorthanded and would have to wait for orders from the white chief to pursue these villains. These young warriors weren't about to wait. They left the reservation and began tracking these killers. Well, it didn't take the Marshal long to realize that these were the same bunch that came through Durango. So, he told the war party how he was on the trail of the same villains and he informed them that he had already killed two in Silverton. He could see that these were indeed just boys, not one of them over 18 and they were not seasoned warriors either, just angry young men. He assured them that he would track, and he would bring to justice each man responsible for these evil deeds and he explained he was the U.S. Marshal in the state and he had all authority to carry out their capture and see to their execution and they needed to leave things in his hands.

Well, after some protest, the young men agreed to head home. They parted their ways and the Marshal continued the hunt. Now it was becoming clear that these men were among the worst Colorado had ever seen and if not caught, they would do more harm as they came upon innocent folks along the trail.

Now Wichita was determined to quicken his pace. After riding all night long in an effort to close the gap between himself and them outlaws. Wichita comes upon the smell of smoke.

Now not fresh burning smoke. But the smoke of embers, old smoke. Strong enough to indicate that something sizeable had burned. He continues to ride towards the smoke and comes upon a cabin partially burned to the ground. He stops about a 100 feet from cabin and he looks the situation over.

The only sounds he hears are birds and rustling of the trees. The cabin set in the middle of the clearing and about thirty or forty feet from the cabin set what looked like an outhouse and then another thirty yards or so from there was a corral. There weren't no livestock, just a stack of straw and some lumber. Instead of walking closer to the cabin, the Marshal moved to the right in order to see around the cabin and as he did, he pulls his Colt and pulls back the hammer. Ready for anything. Satisfied there was no one was around, he approaches the cabin, about fifteen feet from the cabin, there's a ground well. And as he comes closer, he sees a bucket laying on the ground on its side. He takes several more steps and he enters the cabin which is about half there; the rest had been burned down. What Wichita sees makes him sick to his stomach.

A woman lay on the floor, her neck broken and burned from the waist down. These rotten villains had killed and worse… and then they tried to burn the body and cabin. But only half the cabin took to fire. Wind or rain, or something had hindered the flames and put them out. Leaving evidence of the badness of these evil men.

Wichita then holsters his Colt and he walks outside. He then hears a faint cry. It seems to be coming in the direction of the corral. So, he approaches the sound. There he sees a small child hiding in the wood pile. He stops, he kneels down, and he says, "hey, how you doing? My name is Wichita. Look, you see my badge. I'm the U.S. Marshal. Don't be afraid, I've come to help you!" holding out his hand, he says, "come on out. They're gone, they won't be back, I promise!" slowly, the little figure comes out. It's a young boy, about four or five years old. Dirty, no shoes, clothes half torn, and tears running down his face. Wichita continues to hold out one hand and the boy does the same.

He slowly approaches the Marshal, obviously scared, terrified. The Marshal takes his hand, and slowly, gently pulls the boy to his chest. Holding him tight. Thinking of his own boy and overcome with emotion, Wichita closes his eyes, and he gives way to tears.

Now Wichita could see that the boy hadn't eaten in days and he needed some food soon. So, he reached in his saddle bags and handed the boy some jerky. Just to put something in his stomach. He then pulled out his rifle and he went to hunting some meat. About an hour later, he had tasty rabbit cooking on the fire. Well, after eating, the little boy seemed to relax a little. So, the Marshal decides to engage him in a little conversation.

"So, son. What's your name?" "Carson, my name is Carson."

"Really? That's a famous name. Did you know that?" "Nope."

"Well, believe me, it is."

"How old are you, about 8?"

Well Carson kinda raises his head a little, cause he's flattered by the fact that the Marshal thought he was that old and says, "Nooo, I am only five. I just turned five."

"Well, you're big for your age. My boy was much the same." "You got a boy, marshal?"

"I did."

"What happened to him?" "He was killed."

"By bad men, marshal?"

"That's right son. By bad men!" "Carson, where's your pa?

Well Carson sorta bowed his head down and in a quiet, quivery kinda voice he says, "over there."

He pointed to the trees just on the edge of the clearing. The Marshal quickly rose and said, "wait here, son," and went to the spot that he had pointed out. Sure enough, the boy's father lay in the grass, dead, shot in the back, and drug into the trees.

The Marshal takes the boy to the clearing and sets up a temporary camp and tells Carson, "I'll be back in just a little while, son. You wait right here and keep an eye on ol' lucky for me. Would you do that?"

"Okay Marshal. I'll watch him for you."

Then he returns to the cabin, carries the boy's pa, lays him next to his wife and buries them side by side.

Sky Song was the oldest of the three young braves and he was determined to see justice done. Now he believed the words of the white Marshal but he doubted if one man could catch and kill six men and killing was what they needed as far as Sky Song was concerned.

Now Bear, he was the youngest, just fifteen years of age. But truly had the heart and the courage of his namesake. He too had lost his family, but his grandfather had survived. He had always told Bear, "The way of peace is the way of Arapahoe." But in Bear's heart, those words had little meaning today.

Yankee, the third brave, was seventeen years old. He was the quietest of the three, he spoke very little. But like his friends, he was determined to see the white men responsible for the murder of his people face retribution for what they had done. Now the three young braves talked amongst themselves all night long and they decided unanimously rather than return home with no news with the fate of the men who killed their family, and in their eyes, dishonor their loved ones. They would go ahead, catch up with these men, and finish what they had started. For two days and two nights, the Indian war party rode without rest and eventually, caught up to the outlaws on the trail.

Now it was just turning dark and the braves were watching the camp of these three men that they had been hunting. Their horses were tied to the left about twenty feet from the camp fire, still saddled, for that matter. Now they were sure that these were the right men for they recognized the hoof prints of their ponies. Now they could see three bed rolls, they reasoned among themselves. Perhaps the outlaws were asleep. Now little did these young braves realize that these men they were hunting were experienced fighters and even though these men moved carelessly along the trail as if they weren't afraid of anybody following them. They were ever aware of things around them. You see, just before dusk, Tom spotted them Indians on the ridge. Now at first he didn't let on to the others what he had saw, possibly thinking that these were just wandering Indians who'd pay them no mind. But after several hours of being followed, Tom informs Jake and Willy what he had seen. The men decided to make camp and lay in wait in rocks to see if the braves would come on in.

"I see them," says Bear. "There they are, asleep. Now is the time, let's take them."

Sky Song replies, "no, let's move in closer and then attack before they awake."

Yankee, being the more cautious one asks, "why do you think their horses are still saddled? That seems strange to me, maybe we should wait."

Bear in frustration and with impatient anger replies, "no, we must strike now, we will never have a better chance."

Sky Song, on the other hand, agrees with Yankee, "maybe we should wait. This could be a trap."

Just then, Yankee spots one of the men nestled in some rocks. He says to the others, "you see, they are waiting for us. We need to wait."

Suddenly there is a noise behind them. They turn, it's Tom and Jake, both with shotguns.

Now back at the cabin, Wichita had just finished placing markers where Carson's maa and pa had been buried. He spoke some words and then he prepared to leave. Then the Marshal asks, "Carson, you ready to go?"

"Yes sir, I am. But Marshal, where are we going?"

"We are going to find the men who did this to your ma and pa and then I'm gonna find you a place to stay – someplace where you're safe and secure."

Wichita then sets the boy in front of him on the saddle. He puts one arm around him, to hold him secure. Then they head down to the trail.

Now two days had passed on the trail and it was clear where these outlaws were headin. They were headin for Pagosa Springs. Now Wichita figured that the men would hold up there and that he would catch up with them probably by morning but right now, it was about mid-day and the Marshal noticed something different on the trail. New tracks, three, unshod ponies, Indian ponies. "It was the three young braves," he thought to himself. The ones that he had talked to back on the trail some days earlier. Well just then he noticed something else. Some birds, flying in a circle, just a few miles ahead. Now he couldn't quite make out if they were hawks or buzzards, so he quickened his pace. Well, soon it was clear, they were indeed, buzzards. Something or someone was dead or dying.

Now not knowing what he might come across, Wichita sets Carson off the horse and he dismounts himself. "Stay here, Carson. Don't move. I'll be right back, okay?"

"Okay, Marshal, I'll wait for you."

He pulls his Colt, pulls back the hammer and moves towards the spot where the buzzards were hovering. Now as he gets closer, he sees two young braves face down in the dirt and blood… riddled with buckshot. "Where's the third one," he thought to himself. Just then, he notices tracks in the dirt, signs of someone crawling and pulling themselves. He follows the trail and comes upon young Yankee, barely alive.

"Marshal, is that you?"

"Yes, son. It's me. Be still, I am going to get you some water, be still."

Well, he returns, and he holds the boy in his arms and slowly gives him a drink.

"We should have listened, Marshal. But we had to try. Please don't let them get away."

"I promise you son. I promise you I'll find them. You and your brothers, you did all you could. Your people would be proud. Now, rest easy."

Just then, the life breath of the young warrior left and he lay dead in Wichita's arm. Now Wichita returns where he left Carson and he spent the rest of that day preparing to bury the three young braves, the Arapahoe way. Now after laying the last one to rest. Wichita thinks out loud, "I've buried enough folks on this trail. It's time to end this."

He and Carson ride hard all night. Now the sun was rising and the beneath its glow laid Pagosa Springs. Here is where Wichita would bring the fight. His thoughts were no longer of the cabin, nor the young, courageous brave that died in his arms. His mind was fixed on the men that he came to hand out justice to. Fixed on his quest, but still clear headed. First, he would approach the town sheriff, seeking to find Carson, a place to stay and out of harm's way. As the Marshal rides slowly into town, he thinks to himself, "It's gonna be hard to find these men with so many folks in town." He then finds himself in front of the sheriff's office.

"Sherriff, my name is Wichita. From down Durango. I'm the U.S. Marshal."

Well after relaying what had taken place along the trail, with regards to Carson's family and three young braves, as well as the killings in Durango. Wichita asks the sheriff, "have you noticed any strangers coming off the trail, looking like they'd been riding long and hard?"

"Marshal, strangers come in and out of this town so much. I can't say. But my deputy and I, we'll start asking around. By the way, Marshal. Are you the one that killed those two down in the Silverton about a week back?"

Wichita just stood silent.

"They say you fired four shots so fast you couldn't even count them.

Yeah, that's what they say."

But the Marshal still said nothing. He just placed three John Doe warrants on the sheriff's desks and walked out. As Wichita is walking out the door, he stops, turns, he says to the sheriff, "I want you to keep an eye on this boy and keep him out of harm's way. When this is over, I'm gonna find him a place to stay. Some place safe."

Now Wichita gets about ten steps out the door, then Carson runs out, he grabs the Marshal by the leg and he's crying and he says, "Marshal, Marshal, please don't go. Don't leave me alone."

Well the Marshal kneels down, he brushes back Carson's' hair just to get it out of his face and holds him by the shoulders. He looks him in the eyes, he wipes away his tears and then he says, "you'll be fine, son. I won't be far away."

Just then, Carson stiffens up and tears are replaced by a look of downright terror.

"What's wrong, Carson?"

Carson slowly raises his hand and points across the street to a man – a tall, long-haired man. Trail-worn, packing a pistol and a rifle.

"That's him, he's the one."

Wichita motions to the sheriff to take the boy inside. The sheriff does just that. Wichita stands slowly, pulling his Colt, as he rises. He looks in all directions, trying to identify the other two. Streets are so busy, there is too many people to judge who may or may not be the men he's looking for. Then someone yells, "that's Wichita, from Durango."

Now word had already spread all over about what had happened in Durango and the way the Marshal killed them outlaws, shooting them in the heart and throat at the gunfight in Silverton. And folks were already making up wild stories about this Marshal.

Well, hearing this, the outlaw turns to see where the Marshal is and as he turns, he cocks his rifle and he fires, and misses. The Marshal can't return fire, there's too many innocent people running in every direction. The outlaw fires again, this time striking a man in the back, as he passes. Everyone hits the ground, Wichita sees a clear shot. As quick as thought, he raises his shooter and fires one shot, hitting the outlaw in the head.

Just then a shot is fired behind him. The bullet hits the Marshal high in the right shoulder, knocking the .44 out of his hand but instantly, he reaches his left hand out and catches the pistol in midair. Turning and fires, striking the outlaw, center chest. He cocks his pistol and in kneeled position, looks in all directions for the third bandit but he's nowhere to be seen. He returns his gun to the right hand, holsters it, and begins to walk towards the sheriff's office.

Suddenly, a voice calls out from an alley behind him, "not bad Marshal, but you mine."

The cowboy, as he speaks, with his pistol in his hand, raises his gun to fire. Wichita draws, turns, and fires before the outlaw could even pull the trigger. Wichita's bullet, strikes in the abdomen. Knocking him back several feet, stopped only by a hitching post. The Marshal then walks over with his Colt in his hand, and the outlaw coughing, spitting blood, speaks up, "you're a hard man to kill, Marshal."

Wichita looks the outlaw in the eye and says, "no sir, you killed me already."

The outlaw answers, "I ain't never been one for hanging, Marshal." Wichita, pulls the trigger.

Now everyone who had fallen to the ground in fear rose to their feet. Folks hiding behind closed doors come out. All looking in disbelief at the U.S. Marshal that had just killed three men and shocked at the execution of the cowboy who lay at his feet.

The sheriff approaches the Marshal and says, "I'm not sure what happened here today, Marshal. I reckon that gut shot would have killed this outlaw anyway and you killing him again, I reckon it don't make much difference. Besides I figured these men wouldn't have pulled down on ya! if they weren't guilty of something. If they were guilty of half the things you said, well, they deserved what they got. But still Marshal, I hope your business is finished in my town."

"Where can I find a Doctor."

"Over there, cross from the livery. Doc Mills. He'd fix you up."

Well the Marshal walks away, and after a few steps, he turns around and says to the sheriff, "now you take good care of that boy, you hear me. He's a good kid. You take care of him."

Now Doc Mills had been watching the fight after the first shot was fired and he could see the Marshal heading towards his office so he stepped into the street and walked up to the Marshal.

"I'm the Doctor. Let me help you, Marshal." He then leads him to his office.

Well after getting in the office, the Doctor says, "You're a lucky man, Marshal. This bullet hit mostly flesh under your arm. It just nicked a little bit of muscle, you will be fine in a few weeks but till then I'd take it easy with that arm and shoulder."

I've got more to do Doc, I need to be on my way."

"Well, you do what you feel you gotta do. But if you plan on using that Colt anymore, you best give it a rest for couple of weeks. Whoever you're after, they'll wait."

"I suppose your right, Doc. I suppose your right." "Hey Doc, are there any rooms in town."

"Well, I know of at least three."

Well there's a pause, the Doc smiles, Wichita doesn't, but shakes his head, and says, "I guess you're right."

"Now you rest a while, I'll take care of it for you."

Now old Doc Mills walks over to the Harper house and gets the Marshal a room.

"Now who's this for, Doc?"

"It's for the Marshal. The U.S. Marshal from Durango. I'll be bringing him over here a little while later. He needs a couple of days rest."

"Well, you think it's safe for him to be here? I mean, there's been a lot of killing today on account of that Marshal."

"Listen, Jean. He came looking for them outlaws. No one was looking for him. And besides, nobody in their right mind would come after that man after hearing what he did today. I'd never seen anything like that in all my born days."

"Me neither, Doc. Me neither."

Now Wichita had been sleeping for two days straight. I don't care what anybody says, a Colt slug, even if it's a flesh wound, it will put you down for a while. Now, on the third day, he finally came around and he came down out of his room and stepped into the streets. For the past two days, folks had been talking all over town about the gun fight that they had witnessed a few days before. Word had come around also about his run-in with them two bandits in Silverton and as it goes with folks who are scared and full of imagination and tend towards gossip. Everyone in town was either terrified at the sight of the Marshal or they wanted to see him or just be around him hoping to see and hear more from this killing Marshal, as folks had begun to call him. But for the moment, the only interest he had in this town was a little boy named Carson. So, he walked over to the sheriff's office.

"Marshal, I see you're up and around. That's good." "Thanks sheriff, it's good to be up and around."

"Hey I come to check on that boy, Carson. How's he doing? Did you take care of him like I asked you to?"

Well, he then relayed how old Doc Mills had taken the boy in, him and his wife Sarah, and they had promised to take care of him.

"He made me promise to tell you Marshal to stop by his place before you leave, so you could check on the boy."

Well, the Marshal shakes his head and asks, "Where do I find him?" Sheriff gives him direction, he mounts up, and rides out of town,

heading for the Mill's place.

Now, old Doc Mills lived two miles outside of town. Him and his wife Sarah had a small farm—just a large garden.

They had a couple of hogs, milk cows, one of two feeder calves, and some chickens. Just a small family farm.

As Wichita rode up to the Mill's place, he said to himself, "This is a good place; quiet and peaceful. He should be fine here."

Carson, who had been waiting for the Marshal to show up, spots Wichita coming down the trail.

He then hollers, "Marshal! Marshal, you're here!"

Well, Wichita dismounts and the boy jumps, and runs into the Marshal's arms, holding on for dear life.

"You've come to get me, right? We're going together, right?"

Before Wichita could speak, old Doc Mills and his wife, Sarah, call out, "Welcome, Marshal! Come on in."

"Tell me, Marshal, how's that shoulder?"

"Well, thanks to you, I'm as good as new, Doc!"

"Well, hey, let's test it. Let's see you pull that shooter."

Wichita stands and positions his hand to draw, but knowing he's not wholly healed up yet. He just sits down, takes a drink of coffee.

"Listen, Marshal. Why don't you stay here for a couple of weeks? Rest your shoulder, spend some time with the boy; he needs someone he trusts for a while. You're just the man for that job."

"Maybe you're right. I need some rest.

He looks over atCarson, who has a great big grin on his face and he says it again, "Maybe you're right."

Now, for two weeks, Wichita stayed with the Mills. Every day he worked on regaining his strength and speed, in his gun hand , He also spent time with Carson, trying to heal the boy's hurt, all along hurting himself inside as well.

In time, his mind began to focus once again on his quest and the one man he had not caught up with.

He knew by now there was no telling where he might be but no matter how long it took, he was determined he would find him and bring him to justice.

Wichita's days were filled with both peace and restless anxiety. Peace came mostly because of the presence of Carson and the bond between them they had begun to create.

At night, he dreamed of Annie and Luke. The dreams would always start peaceful; serene. But they would wake him up in cold sweat and a horrible feeling of emptiness and anger.

The only way to end this conflict would be to complete his quest and find the last one of the outlaws that killed his family. Only then could he find rest.

Now, the sun was just beginning to come up and like every morning since he arrived at the Mills' place, Wichita rises and saddles his horse to ride a few miles away from the farm and practice, and strengthen his shoulder. Every day, he was getting faster and faster. In fact, it seemed he was getting better and better than before. Maybe it was the pain inside and the emptiness that gave him an edge that he never had before.

But little did the Marshal know that he would soon need such an edge. Now, this day was a little bit different. Unknown to the Marshal,

Carson had followed him and was watching as the Marshal drew, and drew his

pistol; sometimes so fast he could hardly see his hand move.

Carson, watching every move the Marshal made, mimicking those moves, tries to get a little better position, and accidentally knocks over a pile of stones. This catches the Marshal's attention.

Instantly, Wichita turns to the direction of the noise, and levels down with his colt, and then he notices a small figure.

"Is that you, Carson? What are you doing here?"

Carson slowly comes out from around the boulder he had tried to hide behind and he says, "It's just me, Marshal. I hope I didn't scare ya'. I was just wondering what you were doing. I just wanted to be with ya'."

Well, Wichita holsters his colt, he walks over and picks Carson up in his arms.

"Boy, you're getting big. I guess this farm life's good for you.

"Yup, I guess it is, Marshal. But Marshal, I'd rather be with you. I can ride; I can fight; I can be your deputy. Take me with you, Marshal. Please!"

Realizing what was happening and knowing that he must leave the boy behind eventually, the Marshal says, "Listen, Carson. I know you want to come with me but you can't."

Carson begins to cry just a little and says, "But Marshal, why can't I go with you?"

Then setting Carson down and kneeling by his side, Wichita says, "Carson, you know how bad those men were that hurt your ma and pa?"

"Yes, sir."

"Well, there are more men just like that out there. Now, if I don't stop them, they'll hurt more people. People just like your folks. Now I can't let that happen, son. You wouldn't want me to let that happen, would you?"

"No, sir."

"You gotta promise me something, Carson."

While wiping the tears from his eyes and sniffling, Carson asked, "What's that, Marshal?"

"I need you to take care of Doc Mills and Sarah. They need someone to protect them from harm; from bad people just like them outlaws I've been chasin I need you to stay here. I need you to do that for me."

"But I want to go with you."

The Marshal realizing that he has to end this now stands up and in a burst of anger, says,

"I can't take you with me. You'll just be in my way."

Carson looks up with tears, and disappointment on his face. Wichita takes a deep breath and pauses for a moment. He picks Carson up in his arms and fighting back tears, he says, "I can't take care of you, Carson. I just can't. I couldn't even take care of my own son."

He sets Carson on his saddle and they both ride back to the farm, neither one speaking a word.

"Which way ya headed Marshal?"

"Ah back west, maybe towards Durango. I'm hoping to pick up the trail there"

"Marshal. It's been about a month or so. Do you think the trail will be cold by now?"

"Well, there's more than one way to track a man. I'll find him. Just take care of the boy. He means a lot to me."

CHAPTER 3

A Showdown in Dolores

Now, Wichita knew that he had lost much too much time to simply track this bandit down like he had done the rest. It was gonna take some serious thought and some luck for that matter, just to figure out who this outlaw was, what he looked like, and where he was holed up.

No one seemed to know these men, not even the law. Wichita had killed the others before he even had a chance to ask them any questions. "That was stupid," he thought to himself. While riding along the trail, he thought, "Who could identify this outlaw?" And then suddenly, he remembers Charlie Wilson, Sally Wilson's father.

He was there in the bank on the day of the robbery, and it dawned on him, he was also the only survivor who saw these men. He may have heard or seen something that could put him on the right trail. Wichita rides hard back to Durango to speak with Charlie Wilson and prepare himself for a long hard hunt.

Now, I remember that day as clear as can be the day Wichita came back to Durango. I saw him from a distance, much like the first time I saw him, some 12 or 13 years before. He was riding slow, sitting tall in the saddle but this time his friendly smile and disposition was replaced with a cold, hard demeanor, and he looked trail worn and older. Not older in time, but older in life, as if years of living had been snatched from him long before his time.

"Howdy Marshal." "Hey Jed."

"You stayin' a while or just passing through."

"I'm just here to settle some things and to talk with Charlie Wilson. Is he working at the bank today?"

"No, he hasn't been back to the banks since Sally died. He tried one day, but he couldn't even get through the door. He's been home there ever since and he hasn't come out yet."

"I guess things like that take a long time to get over. Time doesn't heal that Jed. Listen, I need a favor."

"Okay, Marshal, what do you need?"

"I need you to saddle me up a pack mule with supplies for a month or so. I need some ammunition for my colt and my winchester, some grub that's right for the trail, and a little whiskey for the cold nights. Gather 'em up and meet me here about noon. Okay, Jed?"

"Sure, Marshal. Consider it done."

Now, we had buried Annie and Luke out at the cabin, and it didn't surprise me that Wichita would ride out to his place first before he talked to Wilson, which is just what he had done.

Now, Wichita arrives at the cabin early in the morning. He rides up slowly looking over the place picturing Annie and Luke. Annie working away in the garden while Luke feeds and waters his pony. He dismounts, ties his horse to the bush just outside the cabin, and walks in. Again, imagining Annie serving dinner. Him and Luke talking and laughing as they did every night before supper, he picks up a picture sitting on a shelf above the fireplace of Annie and Little Luke. One that they had taken some time back when a photographer had come through town and he puts it in his pocket.

Then, he takes some coal oil and pours it all over the cabin. He steps outside and sets the cabin to flames. Coming back, and starting his old life again was not what he had in mind that was plain. He stood and watched the flames for a while, then walked over to Annie's grave and said, "Annie, I don't know if you can hear me. You know I never was much of a believing man, even though you tried your best to make me so, but still, it helps me to talk to you. All my life I looked for you and when I found you, the last thing I ever thought of was losing you, especially like this Annie. I've got one more, and then maybe just maybe I can find my way."

Then, with frustration and anger in his voice and clutching his hat and his hand, he says, "Right now, right now, all I see is making them pay for what they've done. I promise you this, Annie, I won't stop. I won't stop until they're brought to justice. I promise you that."

With that, he rides all the way back to Durango.

Now just on the very edge of town, there were a few houses built when the town was first established. And it was in one of these houses that Charlie Wilson lived. Wichita rides up to the Wilson Place and knocks the door.

Come in, Marshal, I heard you was back in town. Come, come sit.

Would you like a drink?"

Now, Wilson was never much of a drinker, but it was plain to see that that had changed. "No, thanks, Charlie. I just stopped to talk."

"I heard you killed five. Did you… did you find out where the last one is, Marshal?"

"No, I haven't yet, but I reckon he's somewhere around Dolores at least I hope he is."

"Anyway, listen, Charlie, I hate to ask you this, but the truth is, I, I haven't got a clue what this bandit looks like or who he is at all. Fact is he could stand right next to me and I wouldn't know him. I was hoping that maybe you could remember something. Something about them outlaws that might help me. Anything at all. Charlie".

Well, Charlie stood up out of his rocking chair and he walked over to the window. He looked out the window and took a drink of whiskey, and then he said, "Sally was all, I had Marshal since her ma died. She was everything to me. I'll tell you what I remember, I remember her coming into the bank that day and smiling like an angel. I remember her smiling and saying that she just stopped by to say that she loved me, and I… I remember that Marshal. I remember her smile and I hope I never forget it."

And then, he just sits back down, just staring out the window. Well, just when the Marshal was about to leave, figuring that Charlie couldn't help him. Charlie looks up at Wichita and says, "One more thing, Marshal."

Wichita stops, turns, and asks, "What's that, Charlie?"

"That face. The face of the man that shot Sally. How could I have forgotten that? He was laughing Marshal, laughing when Sally fell. He turned and looked at me and he just kept laughing. I, I thought he was gonna kill me too. In fact, I sometimes wished that he had, I remember him clear, he had a scar from his temple to his neck. It looked like a burn of some kind. And one eye was mostly scarred, closed. I remember it clear as can be Marshal, clear as can be."

Well, Wichita began to picture in his mind each one of the outlaws that he had killed. One by one he could see their faces and none had the scar that Wilson had described.

Now he had something to go on finally, and he would waste no time in hunting down this outlaw, no matter where he was. "Thanks, Charlie. Thanks. I'll find him now."

Well, Wichita leaves and heads back to town. He had returned to his office right about noon, just like he had said and I had his pack mule and supplies ready to go.

He had little to say. He came into the office, and looked through some wanted posters, hoping to see a poster that described a scar face bandit with a bad eye so that he could put a name with this outlaw's face. Well, he spent the better part of an hour looking just to come up empty-handed. And it was then that I asked "You coming back, Marshal or what?"

Well, he just stared at the floor for a moment and then he looked up at me and said, "I'm sure it's gonna take a while to track this man down

Jed. After that, I, I'm just not sure. When this is done maybe then I'll know what to do but Jed if you feel like being the Deputy Marshal for a while is too much for you, I'll understand. Just have the town swear in someone to help you until you hear from me."

With that Wichita saddled up, rode outta town heading west, hopefully, to find this outlaw and to find some peace.

Now, while riding down the trail tracking these outlaws, Wichita got to thinking too himself . His only real chance to pick up a warm trail would be to come across someone along the way who had crossed trails with this outlaw and who had lived to tell about it. So far, he'd come across no one . Still, the Marshal would continue to head towards Dolores, just maybe he would find him there. Now, the only problem would be that with the railroad coming thru, there would surely be a telegraph office in town.

And as for the gunfight at Pagosa Springs, word of it would've surely gotten back to Dolores before the Marshal arrived. If the outlaw heard what had happened to his friends, it might spook him or otherwise warn him of Wichita being on his trail, which would be a disadvantage for the Marshal. The fact is that facing disadvantages was something that the Marshal was used to, and so far, his quick hand, and Colt , had met each and every challenge with deadly success.

Then, at about dusk, Wichita smells smoke in the air. He pulls back on the reins and stops for a moment to identify where the smoke is coming from. Then he hears a voice, in the distance.

He can't make out what's being said, but he has a clear sense of the direction that it's coming from. He dismounts, ties his horse, and packed a mule to a tree. He pulls his colt, slowly cocks the hammer back, and quietly walks toward what the Marshal expects to be someone's camp.

Now there in the trees, he sees an old man. He had the look of a Tin Pan , an old prospector. He had an old worn-out hat bent back in the front so that he could see good when looking for gold and bent down in the back to keep his neck from burning due to being in the mountain sun for long days panning hour after an hour. As the Marshal got closer, unnoticed by the old timer, more than likely because he was making so much noise, he couldn't hear a herd of buffalo. The Marshal could see his face clear. He had a rough beard speckled with gray hair. He had a pair of round rim spectacles and squinty eyes. He had a high-pitched voice. He wore overalls with a long sleeve shirt, and a bright red bandana wrapped around his neck. He was about average height, but he was thin, gangly looking. Now, there was a time when lone prospectors, like this old timer, were plentiful in these parts, but there were fewer and fewer these days due to the big mining companies moving in and mining gold by tons instead of by pan fulls.

What was odd though, was that the old man was sitting by a fire and there weren't a horse or packed mule anywhere in sight. No bed roll , no sign of any possibles, just this old prospector, clearly upset about something, poking at a fire and talking to himself, cursing and swearing. "That no good polecat , If 'n I was 10 years younger, I'da showed him what fer"

Well, the Marshal approaches slowly, and when he's about talking distance, he hollers , "Hey, old timer."

Well, the old prospector who was sitting on a fallen log was so surprised and startled. He gives out a Yelp. "Wow." In an attempt to jump to his feet, he falls back off the log.

Unfortunately, the stick he was poking the fire with had caught on fire and in the excitement had gone flying in the air. And what goes up comes down right in the front of the old timers' pants. Well, he tries to put out the flames, but he just manages to catch his pants on fire. Wichita runs to his aid and throws dirt on the old prospector's pants.

And then he says, "You all right, old timer. I didn't mean to spook ya" "Spook me. You pert near burned me to death. Dad blame ya"

Well, standing up. He says something else, but it was mumbled and under his breath. And I imagine it, it weren't too nice. Well then, the Marshal asked, "Where's your horse or your mule old timer. Did you lose e"m?

"No, I didn't lose my mule. It, along with everything else I own was stolen by some low down Sidewinder Day before yesterday. He'd a killed me too if 'n I hadn't jumped in the river back at piece . Yes sir. He'd a killed me for sure."

"Well, was this bandit alone? No sir. If,n he was alone, I'd a whooped him on the spot. Dad blame sidewindin varment. fact was he had four others with him. They had the look of hard-desperate men"

"I see you carry a badge US Marshal. You looking for these bandits Marshal."

"Well, that depends. Did you happen to notice any of them men carrying a scar on their face?"

Well, the old timer takes off his hat and scratching his balding head.

He says "A scar huh, Well, let me think."

Well, Wichita turns stepping in the direction that he left his horse and pack mule, he takes a few steps, and the old timer says, "You mean like a burn Marshal? Kind of a across the side of his face and one eye"

Wichita stops and turns. "That's exactly what I mean. Did you see this man"

"He's the pole cat that tried to kill me. The others just watched and

laughed. I, I reckon he was a leader of that bunch."

Well, Wichita thinks to himself, how could this outlaw be so close? It had been a month or so since he had come across the split in the trail. Where'd this bandit go and why hadn't he high tailed it to Dolores by now.

Now, what the Marshal didn't know was that a bunch of boys had come out of New Mexico on the run from the law after robbing a freight office in Santa Fe.

Once they crossed the state line, the posse on their trail had to let 'em go, and they did. Now the plan was this. One Eye Jack McPherson was gonna hit the bank in Durango with old Tom Jenkins, which they did. Then he would split up, ride hard to Dolores and find out if the miner's payroll was indeed due to come in on the railroad, and then he would meet his own gang back in Cortez problem was these boys just couldn't stay out of trouble, and they had to leave Cortez like they did New Mexico and in a hurry.

Now in the Mesa Verde area, there are miles and miles of old Indian ruins in the cliffs . There's still a few Navajo there, but they're peaceful enough. You leave them alone and they'll leave you alone.

Well, these here ruins are a good place to hide. Now ol' Jack McPherson spent some time in Dolores and then made his way to Cortez to meet up with his gang. But when he got there, he found his gang was on the run, not knowing just where the boys would be and finding out there was indeed a huge payroll in cash due in Dolores. Well, he went to looking for 'em. He made his way to the ruins figuring that that's where they'd be. But he found that their tracks led back east towards Durango. It was on that trail Old One Eye finally found the gang laying low, figuring that the law from Cortez was on their trail. It was shortly after that that they came across the old timer who just happened to have a mule, food, and water, and the rest is history.

Fact is these boys may be good at killing, but they were lousy at planning and that was a fact that cost them plenty in time and much, much more. Wichita asked the old timer, "How long since you last seen these men."

"This morning, Marshal. This morning."

"I thought you said that they stole your pack Mule sometime back."

"That's right. But I followed e'm, hoping I could steal back my mule. But by the time I caught up with e,m I was so tuckered out, I, I just hid the trees and waited for 'em to leave. I had no gun or nothing, so I just let 'em go."

"Which way did they head old timer?

"West. They headed West Marshal. I heard 'em say that they were figuring they'd rob the bank in Dolores. This time of year, the railroad brings in a lot of cash to pay the men working for them big mining companies, you know, down there along the divide. Them other boys come from up Mesa Verde. They'd been holding up in them Indian rooms. Heard e"m say they killed a minor and tried to take his gold, but they didn't get much. They were pretty upset about that too. Reckon their need'in to hit that bank about now"

"Old timer, you take my mule and head for Dolores. I'm riding hard and I don't think you can keep up." Well, the old prospector was a little upset, and the Marshal could tell he was a little irritated at the insinuation that he can't keep up cause he was old. Wichita says, "Of course, I mean the mule can't keep up."

And with that, the old timer says, "Don't worry. I'll take good care of your mule, and I'll catch up with you in town."

Wichita hits the saddle riding hard all night long. He'll catch up with this bunch before the bank opens in the morning. Facing this scar faced outlaw was all that he could think of.

Now, Wichita had just reached the top of the ridge just east of Dolores. The sun was rising behind him, and as the sun spread light on the valley and the town below, Wichita sat in the silhouette. He pulled his colt, checking to make sure it was fully loaded, and then holstered his gun.

The blood thirsty villain that had murdered Annie Luke, little Sally was at the base of the ridge. Now the fact was just as Wichita thought might happen, the news of the killings in Silverton and Pegosa Springs had reached folks in Dolores through the telegraph. Talk was that Wichita; the US Marshal had set out on a hunt for six bandits with killin on his mind. And as stories often do, the account of the gun fight in Silverton and the springs by now had grown into an account of a blood thirsty Marshal bent on revenge and any who may get in his way would suffer the same fate. So, it was no surprise that as Wichita rode through town that morning, men, women, and children that were out on the streets, all hid behind closed doors, fearing someone was about to die that day, leaving no one on the street.

Now, on the opposite end of town, the outlaws were gathered together planning to hit the bank, just as the bank owner opened the doors in the morning. They had arrived in town late the night before but instead of hitting the saloon as they normally would've. Ol' One Eye Jack McPherson insisted that they'd get a good night's sleep so they could hit the bank at first light.

Now, the gang had not heard the stories about the Marshal, nor the fact that he was on his way to Dolores. But Old One Eye Jack heard the news when he first got town a few weeks before. He figured this Marshal had just gotten lucky somehow, and he wasn't too worried about another law man. He killed plenty before, this one would be little trouble for as far as he was concerned. But he wasn't about to let on to the other boys figuring they might get spooked and turned tail and all that cash would be lost. If indeed the Marshal showed , Jack figured, ah, he might kill two or three, but there was no way he could take 'em all.

Now, Wichita was focus as he rode in to town.

His only thought was of taking down the outlaw and if need be, those that were with him. The look on his face was hard and cold. A look of complete determination. In fact, it was a look that served to only fuel the stories that folks had heard about Him.

The Marshal first , as always, always stops in front of the sheriff's office, steps off his mount, and he approaches the door. But the sheriff is gone either by circumstance or by choice. The Marshal looks up and down the street trying to spot them outlaws or the bank, cause he knows that's where he'll find the men that he's after. About then, the owner of the bank opens the door unaware that the bandits were moving in behind him. One Eye pulls a hunting knife and puts it to the banker's throat. "You scream, I'll cut your head off now. Take me to the vault. Now open it." Well, the bank owner does just what he's told. Jack then orders his men, "Billy, you and James get that money. And then let's get outta here quick before anyone comes in."

Now it was about 8:45 in the morning and the bank didn't open for business till 10. If the bandits could get in and out in time, no one would know for an hour or so that the bank had even been robbed.

Billy and James filled the saddlebags with the cash and then two others would tie them to the saddles of the horses that were tied just outside the bank. Frank, one of the bandits outside, notices a lone man on the early morning street. It was Wichita, the Marshal notices him as well. Frank says, "Hey Jack, I think we got the company out here. Come take a look"

At that, Jack pulls the knife across the bank owner's throat. He falls to the ground, bleeding to death, not able to yell for help. Well, Jack steps towards the door, but he stays just inside the doorway so as not to be seen.

By this time Wichita's badge is plain to see. Some say the sun was shining off of it.

"It's the law," says Frank, "What do we do, Jack?"

"Well, there's five of us boys and only one of him. What do you think we do? We kill him." One Eye Jack and his gang step into the street. They figure they'll kill this Marshal and ride outta town. Simple as that, but it wouldn't be that simple.

Wichita steps in to the middle of the street standing squarely facing the outlaws with his hand positioned ready for the fight, Jack speaks first. "You must be the Marshal. I heard killed five of my compadres."

Wichita notices Jack has a clear scar on the side of his face covering most of one eye. This is the man that he'd been looking for the last of the outlaw band that murdered his family with his heart pounding and fighting to keep his calm so as not to make a foolish move, Wichita answers with contempt and hatred in his voice, "You must be the ugly yellow back shooting coward that murdered my family."

Jack, clearly affected by the intensity of the Marshal and with uncertainty in his voice replies, "You may be fast Marshal, but you can't take us all."

All five men fan out, all with their hands positioned for the fight, and they were all clearly afraid.

One or two, repeat. "He can't take us all." "No way. He can't take us all."

Wichita speaks up. "Maybe I can't boys." But then looking right in the eyes or the EYE of Jack McPherson, he says, "But you, you'll be the first one to fall.

Now what happened next is hard to say. Some say it sounded like there was only one shot fired, one shot, five men dead. Some say a couple of the outlaws got spooked and ran, and Jack killed them as they was running.

And the Marshal shot the rest, including Jack. But these are the facts, all five men were shot in the heart, none in the back. As for Jack, he was shot in between the eyes and in the heart. Five bandits, five men dead, six bullet holes.

Well, when the smoke cleared, Wichita walks over to One Eye Jack's body and he places a John Deere warrant on his chest.

Then someone said, they heard him saying, "It's finished, Annie, now you can rest." He then reloads a six gun and he rides out of town.

Now, the town folks, they buried them outlaws, but didn't know who they were, so they just laid them side by side in a grave, and they put a marker on it and it read. "Unknown outlaws killed the day Wichita came to town." Now, it wasn't till later that they learned who these outlaws were, but they just left the grave marked as it was, and it's that way to this day.

CHAPTER 4

The Old Timer's Cabin

Now Wichita, heading back down the trail to Durango, hadn't gotten too far when he spotted the old prospector riding his pack mule coming towards him. As they approached each other, they slowed down to a stop. At first, neither one of them said a word. They just nodded to each other. Then the old timer, spoke up.

"I take it you found them outlaws Marshal. Did you stop 'em from robbing that bank?"

Wichita answers "Yes old timer. I stopped 'em, I stopped 'em Permanent."

"Well, where you headed now, Marshal?"

"I ain't sure any place but Durango, just somewhere that I can rest."

"Listen. I got me a cabin just outside of Telluride. I was headed there when them pole cats ambushed me. I got a little mine there, it ain't much, but it keeps me alive and I reckon it'll last a while. Nobody knows about it but me. Why don't you ride up there with me and rest yourself a while, least ways till you figure out what you're going to do."

"That sounds good old timer. That sounds really good." And the two of them ride off to Telluride.

Now, Wichita and the old prospector, rode for days through Rock Mountains and with the exception of a few traveling miners moving from one gold strike to another, which was common in them days, their days on the trail were uneventful. Wichita found that the company of the old timer was welcome and his stories that he would tell at night while they sat around a campfire fixing vittles and coffee , well, they were entertaining and pretty far fetched for that matter, still they brought some peace to Wichita's mind and his heart. Wichita was fast developing a close relationship and a good friendship with this crazy old man as he sometimes referred to him.

That was something that he needed right now.

Still, at night, he would dream of Annie, little Luke and the life that they had together. But all too often, the dreams would end up in nightmares, and Wichita would wake up with a renewed determination to hunt down, and bring to justice any who would come into Colorado with the intent upon robbin', killin', and hurtin' innocent folks, those under what the Marshal considered to be his charge.

Wichita was determined to never fail again, as at least in his mind, he had failed his sweet Annie.

Sittin by a fire the old timer asked.

"Wichita, where'd that name come from? Ain't nobody give that name to a child on purpose unless maybe you was born there or something."

"No old timer. I wasn't born with there. I just picked it up years ago, passing through dodge."

"Well, what happened, Marshal?"

Well, Wichita relays the story of how he had come to Dodge, a young Pinkerton detective on the trail of some bandits that had been stealin and killin along the railroad, taking payrolls, robbin passengers and such. He was to meet some other detectives all working undercover in Dodge and then make their way to Wichita where he had a lead that the outlaws would strike again.

Now while sitting in the Long Branch, a fight broke out between a few cowboys, over some saloon gal. At first, it was just fist a flyin and chairs a breakin. Well, eventually someone informed the town Marshal what was going on, a fella named Masterson. And, he wasn't one to put up with such mischief, especially from drunken cowboys. Now, the law in Dodge at the time was that no one was to wear a side arm into town. That was a law that old Masterson invented himself.

And the young detective being a law-abiding citizen figured he'd better let the Marshal know that he was in town and why, mostly so he could keep his gun, which in those days was kept under his coat it was a short barreled colt.

Well, Masterson gave him permission to keep the colt, but he told him not to start any trouble less-in he tells him first.

Now, the young detective's first instinct was to step in and stop the fight between the cowboys, but he had no way of telling the Marshal. And besides, there were four them and one of him. Anyway, no one had any guns.

Well, about that time, Masterson comes in the Long Branch with his pistols and a shotgun. He demands that the cowboys stopped their fighting.

Well, they stopped alright but then just as the Masterson turns his back to walk out of the saloon, leaving the cowboys with just a warning, which was unusual for Masterson. Two of the men pull knives outta their boots and raise their hands about to throw them into the Marshal's back. In an instant, the young Pinkerton detective pulls his shooter and fires two shots, hitting both men in the hand.

Well, Masterson turns, he levels down that shotgun and fires at them cowboys hitting both buckshot, but not killing either one. Masterson asked the young man who had saved his life to come to the office. And then after locking up them two cowboys and sending for the doc, Masterson asked the young man, "What be your name, son."

"I'd rather not say. I'm on the trail of some bandits for the railroad. I don't wanna take a chance Someone might hear my name. I'm kind of known on the railroad, and if someone slipped it, I might lose my edge. And with the telegraph that's something I'm concerned about."

"Fair enough."

"Where you headed? I'm headed to Wichita. I'm supposed to meet some other detectives there, we gotta lead that's where these bandits are gonna hit next."

"Fair enough. I'll just call you Wichita. And Son, thanks for saving my life."

"Well, that's quite a story, Marshal. So, you just kept that brand from then on, right?"

"Yep, that's right. Just stuck. I've kept it ever since." "So, what's your real name?"

"Well, after I left the Pinkertons, the only one I ever told that to would be Amy. I figured that will stay between her and me."

"I understand."

Now, early the next morning, Wichita, the old prospector, had arrived at the cabin.

Now it was a small place, big enough for one to fit comfortable, but two could make do if need be. It sat deep off the beaten path in a thickit of trees, pines and aspen, and there was an outhouse, a one holer.

It had a root cellar, and a spring ran year-round, just a few yards from the cabin.

The cabin was strong and good for holding up in the winter time and winter in the Rockies would be coming soon. Now Wichita decided that he would stay with the old man for a while, at least until the end of the first bad snow and then he'd head back down to Durango. Where he'd either resign as Marshal or he'd get back to taking care of business, dealing with bandits, villains, and desperate men his way.

The fact is Wichita was mellowing out a little, but he was still determined to rid Colorado of the kind of murderous scum such as the men he had handed out justice to these past weeks.

Wichita asks, the old man. "Hey, did you build this cabin?"

"Sure did son did it my own self, about 10 year ago. She's a fine structure, don't you think?"

"She sure is old man. She sure is."

Now it was about the middle of December and Wichita and the old prospector had spent many a week together talking about things, things the Marshal hadn't talked to anyone about since Annie and Luke died. They also spent time working together in the old man's mine, hunting, fishing, gathering wood for the winter.

The old man would tell stories growing up in the south where he had a dozen brothers and sisters, even more cousins, as he would put it, aunts and uncles, as the old timers said, "Plum too many folks that I knew too well," So he headed to the Rockies, he fancied himself after men like Bridger and Kit Carson said he even had a little Jeremiah Johnson in him.

Well, the truth is the old man had the heart to be a mountain man. There weren't no doubt about that, and he could spin yarns as good as any mountain man ever did, but he got the gold fever once and he never got rid of it. Spent most of his life panning for gold and never really had a strike that amounted to much more than what he needed to start looking for another.

Now, that was a common story amongst old time panhandler's back in the day.

Now Wichita saw this old man as something far more than just an old pan handler. He had thought about just staying with the old timer, and take care of him. He could see he was getting tired and long in the tooth for mountain life and digging for gold

And there was a real peace about the place. It helped the Marshal not to completely forget, but not to think about Durango every hour of every day.

Now, that night was an uncommonly cold one, and Wichita brought in extra firewood that whole day. "Hey, old man, when was the last time you seen a night this cold this time of year."

"Well last time was, let me think, ……. back in 53, why it was so cold I went out and killed me two grizzlies that very night. Only had one shot to do it with to.

My powder for my Hawkins was damp and I had already left the cabin, so I waited until two Grizzlies were side by side. Then I fired one shot from my 50 caliber and it hit the first one in the head, passed on through and struck the other one in the head. Don't you know? Well, I skinned them critters that night and made myself two blankets. I was warm that night and the rest of that winter.

"Well, what'd you do with them blankets Old man, we could use 'em?" "Traded 'em I did, that spring for a new mule."

Wichita smiles and he says, "That's quite a story old man, quite a story. Old timer, how about putting another log on that fire since you traded them blankets? We need it."

Now. It was so cold that even the critters were looking for shelter. Unknown to the old man and Wichita, a diamond back rattler had made his way into the cabin. It curled up underneath the logs figuring it would hibernate there, I guess. When the old timer bent over to pick up a log, the snake struck, hit'in the old man, in the throat .

Wichita reacts instantly, he throws a cleaver sitting on the table just a few inches away and it kills the snake, but it's too late for the old man.

He picks up the old timer and he lays him on the bed. The snake had hit a main artery and the poison had already started running through his body.

"Old timer, it's my fault. I, I should have seen him sooner. I'm sorry. I'm so sorry." The old man grabs the Marshal's shirt and raises up and speaking in anger he says, "You listen to me. It wasn't your fault. Don't you dare let me go under thinking you blame yourself for this too. You blame yourself for everything son, for Annie, little Luke and those folks in Durango, you gotta let it go."

Well, the old timer, then let's go of the Marshal's shirt and he just falls right back into the bed. Exhausted, and with life about to leave him, the old timer says, "I wanted to tell you this for a long spell, but I was afear'ed you'd get mad and leave. I didn't want that. But that don't matter now, until you realize you can't blame yourself for all the badness in this here world you ain't never going to be free, free to be the man that you really are. The man you were before Annie died, and I gotta feeling that was a good man."

"Ah, just take it easy old man. You're gonna be all right."

"I'm the one that spins the yarns here, son, you and I both know better than that. Now you bury me deep, you hear. I don't want any wolves digging me up. And don't you burn down this cabin. It's yours. She's a good cabin. She'll shelter you when you need it."

Well, the old man coughs and he can hardly talk now, but he does say, "I ain't said this enough in my life, but I'm a needing to say it now. I got deep feelings for you son, if you get my meaning. Just like you was kin… my own boy."

Wichita, seeing that his friend was about to pass, says, "I love you too, old man."

And with that, the live breath of the old man left. And Wichita wept.

CHAPTER 5

The Last Hunt, Carson and The Asley Boys

Now, Wichita did indeed return to Durango. In fact, over the next 10, to 12 years or so, he'd return often. Most of the time though, where he was and what he was doing, no one knew. When he did come to town, it was only long enough to resupply with ammunition and other needs and things, and then he'd stop and check at the office on new wanted posters for desperate and dangerous villains.

When the Marshal came to town, he would talk very little, but he would, up until he passed on, visit Annie's father William and ask how certain folks were doing such as myself and Charlie Wilson that was little Sally's father and a few others. When he left town, he'd go straight to the old place where Annie and Luke were buried and he'd spend some time there.

Then he would hit the trail and hunt down outlaws. Now songs were writ and stories were told about this law man, Wichita, and how he had faced down a hundred outlaws. Truth is, in his whole life, he hunted down, oh, maybe 40 and if they let him, he brought every one of 'em back for trial, that was for sure and for certain, but the stories were told over and over and a legend was born.

There was this one story though, that happened just about 10 years or so after Annie died, and they say that it was the last time that Wichita ever hunted down an outlaw. After that, he simply disappeared for years. It's a story worth telling, and it goes like this.

Now, a young cowboy in his late teens had gotten tired of life as a cowboy on the range in Eastern Colorado, and he decided he'd take an easier way. That way was the way of the outlaw.

He wore a set of pearl handled shooters, had gotten pretty good at the quick draw. He had gotten used to and enjoyed the attention he got from other cowboys and especially city slicker's whenever he crossed their paths and would show off his skills.

Now, one day he walked into a small bank in Lyman, Colorado, and after pulling his pistol, he demanded that the teller fill his saddle bags with money.

Well, the teller did just what he was told, but just as the cowboy turned to leave, the teller pulled out his own gun from underneath the counter and shot at the cowboy, but he missed . The cowboy, in turn, turned, drew his pistol, and fired, hitting the teller in the heart. Well, he left town on the run with about $800. That was more money than he'd ever seen in his whole life.

Well, he rode hard for a whole day and got away clean as far as he could tell. Well, they say he was heading for Leadville,

To see a gal, but stopped in Denver for a few days, and there he got into a scrape with a trail boss and shot him, again, leaving town in a hurry.

Well, posters were put out on this cowboy and Wichita picked up on one while he was in Buena Vista, that was a wild mining town about 60 miles south of Leadville, known for its many saloons and a place where desperate and hardened villains would hold up. Well, he began to read the poster and it described the cowboy as in his late teens and went by the name of Luke.

Now, it was well known in these parts that Wichita's family had been killed when his own son named Luke was about 10 years old. When the Marshal first seen the poster and read about this young outlaw, at first, he thought about how this boy and his son would've been about the same age. And with this being the first time he'd ever tracked down such a young man, he couldn't help but ponder on the possibility of how someone the age of his own son could die at his hand.

Now, that was a thought that truly troubled the Marshal.

But still, out of duty, as he had done many times before, the Marshall saddled up and headed out after this young lone out law.

Well, the story is that he trailed him to Dillon , and it was there that Wichita's life would change forever. And this is what happened.

It seems a cowboy had a gal in Leadville that he fancied and figured with Leadville being such a populated town in them days, he'd just hold up with her, get lost in the crowd, and hide from the law if 'in it came looking for him.

Now, the problem was that this little gal that he thought so much of, didn't think much of him, least ways, not as much as she did the reward money that was on his head.

So, when he showed up in Leadville, she informed the local sheriff that he was there. Now, the sheriff was a good man, ain't no doubt about that but he had just recently had an accident and he wrenched his back. He could hardly walk, much less stand up in a fight, and he wasn't looking forward to facing down a wild young cowboy who may or may not be any good with a colt besides, he had the telegraph at his disposal.

So, he decided to let the US Marshal deal with this young killer. Well, after some days with Wichita closing in on Leadville, having been tipped off where this outlaw was holed up, word came to the outlaw, thru someone who knew him and knew of Wichita's reputation, that the law was coming.

Well, immediately the cowboy saddled up and headed north.

In fact, just hours before Wichita arrived in Leadville. Well, the Marshal continued hot on the trail of this bandit who had killed at least two. The young man had been riding hard. His horse was badly lathered, and he could go no further. So, the outlaw decided to stop in Dillon to water and rest his horse and do the same for himself.

Now, there was a certain look that gun fighters had in them days, and it wasn't from the clothes they wore or the guns they toted. Some would dress, with fancy vests and hats, and some carried two guns, some just one.

Some turned backwards for the cross draw, and some wore concealed weapons, some just a pistol in their belt no holster. No, it wasn't these things that gave one away as a gun fighter. It was something else. A look in the eyes, the way they carried themselves with a chip on the shoulder, arrogant, bold.

And then some, as this young outlaw, who wanted people to know what they were. They were notches on the handles of their shooters.

Well, as the young man entered into the streets of Dillon , folks all around took notice. He came in fast, kick'in up, plenty of dust.

Just in front of the town saloon was a watering trough and a hitchin post. The young man tied his horse to the post, given the animal just enough slack to reach the trough.

He then walked through the swinging doors of the saloon.

Now, inside the saloon were about a dozen men, miners and town folk, and there was two or three saloon gals and a bartender. There was quite a bit of talking going on amongst the folks in the saloon until one or two of the miners noticed the young man's colts.

He had two and each one had notches on the handles, and he wore them guns somewhat low so that he could pull them shooters quick with minimal movement. Well, after bringing to the attention of others, the notches on the cowboys' pistols, the folks in the saloon quieted down.

Some, figured trouble was about and even left. Well, others stayed, they were figuring that maybe they'd see a gun fight. Well, they were about to see just that. The young cowboy says to the bartender, "Bartender, give me a whiskey and I mean now." Well, the bartender pours the young outlaw a glass. "You look like you could use one son. Where you from?"

The cowboy just looks up at the bartender and drinks down his drink looking the bartender straight in the eyes, as if to say none of your business. He then says "Another," and the bartender pours another drink, this time saying nothing. He just backs off. Well, just before swallowing the drink down, the cowboy says to himself but out loud where everybody can hear it, "I've run all I'm gonna run,today, one of us will be dead."

At that moment, the saloon doors swing open, Wichita stands in the door. He looks at the boy and says, "Is your name, Luke."

"What's it to ya Marshal."

Well, the Marshal couldn't help but think about how his son would be the same age as this young outlaw and if 'in he killed this boy, he wasn't sure he could live with that. He asked the boy, "Do you wanna live, son? Cause I'm taking you in and it's up to you alive or laying over your saddle dead."

The young gun fighter hardened and bitter and bound and determined to make a name for himself. He simply shakes his head and he pulls his colts. Wichita hesitates and the outlaw's bullet barely misses Wichita, but then instantly a loud blast a long muzzle flame. The young outlaw lay dead on the saloon floor. Slowly Wichita walks over to the outlaw. He bends down and looks for a moment at the young man thinking to himself, "What a waste of life."

Then he says out loud, "There's been enough. I'm through." He takes off his badge, lays it on the young Outlaw's chest, and he walks out the door. Now, that was the last outlaw that Wichita would ever hunt down.

Now just outside of Pegosa Springs at the Small Family Farm of Old Doc Mills and his wife Sarah. Carson, now about 16 years old, taller than most grown men, standing about five foot eleven, slim with light brown hair and bright blue eyes. He had just had another fight with Sarah, another of many in the last year or so.

It seems a new family had moved into the area and they had two sons just a few years older than Carson. The problem was these boys were real trouble. In fact, the family had moved from New Mexico mostly to get away from the law. You see, the boys had been caught stealing on a few occasions and the last time the circuit judge issued a warrant for both boys but the family left New Mexico before the local law could catch up with him.

The boys, Pa was a lazy ex-army man and he had a pretty seedy past of his own. Trouble just followed this family everywhere they went and them and trouble found their way to Carson.

Now, Carson walked out to the barn, angry with Sarah cause she refused to let him go to town with the Asley boys. She could see plane that these boys were no good. The problem was Carson was full of curiosity about town and saloons and pool halls and the like. And since old Doc Mills died, Sarah was having a real difficult time keeping a handle on the boy.

Sarah knew Carson wasn't a bad boy, but he was bitter. And from time to time, verbally angry over what had happened to his folks and how at least the way he saw the law had let him down, first, by not protecting his family and second, by leaving him alone, meaning Wichita. For years, he waited for him to return, but he never did.

Each year, he became more and more disappointed until hope became replaced with anger and resentment. Feelings that Carson was just too young to understand or to deal with for that matter.

Carson asked Joey Asley, "Are you coming or not? Don't tell me Old Lady Mills has still got you wrapped around her finger. You ain't never gonna amount to anything unless you do something about that boy."

"I know. It's just that." "It's just what"

Carson pauses and then he says, nothing. "Let's go ."

For several weeks, the Asley brothers have been talking about how easy it would be to steal the strong box off the stage line when it stopped every month in Pagosa Springs on its way to South fork to pay the men working at the lumber mills.

Frank, the oldest brother, worked a few days a month feeding the horses for the stage line and cleaning the stage coach and so forth while passengers would take a rest and get fed at the station on the edge of town. Frank had, on several occasions, seen the strong box and could have easily, with a little bit of help, taken it unnoticed.

Well, times were hard for the Asley boys in them days like it was for many. And the boys like Their Pa were disinclined to hard work and just making do. So, the boys devised a plan to rob the stage, but not in the conventional way, and here's what their plan was. Frank had quit his part-time job a week before, so as to eliminate suspicion, claiming he had to stay with his pa day and night for a few weeks to help him get through a sick spell.

Now with Frank being gone for a week or so and folks thinking he was home with his brother and Pa , the boys would hide out in the station the night before the stage carrying the payroll came in. When the morning stage came through and everyone was busy eating and resting from the stage ride, the boys would grab the strong box, then high tail it back to the farm before anyone knew what had happened.

Then the stage would leave and it would be days before anyone knew the payroll was even missing. Simple as that, seemed like a good plan. Problem was they needed both of them to get the strong box. One to hold the back cover of the stage open. It was pretty heavy and then one to grab the payroll box. That left no one to look out for any who might unexpectedly come by.

Well, that's where Carson came in.

That night, all three boys put their plan into action. Everything was going just as planned except for one unexpected turn of events.

Now, it had been agreed between Carson and the Asley boys that there would be no firearms.

Carson insisted that the only way that he would help would be if no one got hurt. Well, Frank was reluctant to agree, figuring that if someone caught him in the act and he had a gun, at least he could get away and if needed, shoot his way out. But Carson was needed, and if it took an empty promise to get his help, well then an empty promise is what he would get.

Frank put a small derringer in his boot and he had every intention of using it if it was necessary. All of this was unknown to Joey and Carson. Now, Joey was holding the door to the back compartment of the stage coach and Frank had both his hands on the strong box. Carson was standing by the door leading to the stage house where folks ate and rested up for the next stretch to South Fork, that way, if anyone was to come in, they figured that it would be from that direction. Unknown to them was the fact that Sarah, had noticed that Carson hadn't come home all night and she was afraid that he was with them Asley boys. So, having a feeling that something no good was up. She decided to go to town early that morning and find Carson.

Now, as she rode her buggy into town, she noticed Carson's horse tied at the back end of the stage station. She also recognized Joey and Frank's horses, and she figured that she'd find them boys there. Joey says, "Hurry up. We gotta get outta here fast. This thing's heavier than I thought it was."

It was just then that the strong box slips out of Frank's hands and falls, and then for some reason it opens up, and paper and silver spill out all over the ground.

From out of nowhere. The boys here, "What do you think you boys are doing?" Frank, in a panic with his back to whoever it was, pulls the derringer, turns and fires hitting Sarah in the heart, killing instantly.

Carson hearing the shot, runs into the stage area and he says, "What are you idiots doing? I said, no guns."

At that instant, Carson sees Sarah lying dead on the floor.Joey runs to Carson, "Carson, let's go or we're dead men." He grabs his arm and says, "Come on Carson. Now". Carson responds,

"Get away from me. Leave me alone." Then he tries to revive Sarah.

Frank and Joey run out the back door, leaving Carson alone. Well just then passengers, the stage driver, and the station manager entered to see what all the commotion was. As they enter, they see Sarah dead on the floor. Carson leaning over her and the cash from the strong box on the ground. Three of the passengers along with the stage driver, immediately subdue Carson who is in shock at what just happened, Sarah, the only mother Carson has known for over 10 years lay dead, and he thinks to himself, "It was my fault." He simply could not speak. They walked him to the sheriff's office, where the sheriff locks him behind bars.

Now, Sheriff John Macy had known Carson for over six years ever since he moved to the Springs and was appointed sheriff. He was very close to Sarah and old Doc Mills . In fact, Sarah and John, since the Doc died, had become close friends and talked many times about the difficult times Carson was going through and the concern that Sarah had for the boy. Being he was the law in town he also was aware of the Asley boys and their reputation. And even though there wasn't anything he could hold him on here, he, like most folks around, saw the boys as trouble just waiting to happen. And he knew that Carson and them boys were being seen together more and more often.

Well, speaking to Carson, the sheriff asked, "Son, you wanna tell me what happened here?"

Carson looking through the bars of the window in the back of the cell. At first, he just says nothing, just looks down and shakes his head, and he begins to cry. "I told him, no guns. No one was to get hurt, especially Sarah."

He turns and looks at John Macy. "I loved her sheriff. She was all I had. How could this happen?"

The sheriff then asks Carson, "Who shot Sarah? I want you to tell me who shot Sarah son."

Carson trying to get control of himself says . "Frank, it was that lousy lyin' Frank, he shot her"

"Where they headed son? "To the farm and then south I, I think Arizona."

"Okay son."

In less than 20 minutes, 20 men were ready to ride. The posse caught up with the boys at the farm just as they were leaving. They had delayed their escape trying to get enough supplies together to get them over the trail. Far enough from Pegosa Springs to be safe. They hadn't planned for a quick getaway figuring no one would know for at least a few days that the stage had even been robbed.

Seeing the posse approaching the farm and hoping to give them boys a head start. Old man Asley fires on the posse wounding one man, but he was shot dead seconds after his first shot.

The boys gave up without a fight. They were brought back to town and they were put in separate cells.

Now to say the least, Sarah was very much loved and respected in and around Pagosa Springs.

Sarah and her husband, Doc Mills, had been helping folks around these parts for decades, and the men responsible for the death of Sarah would not get off lightly that was for sure, and for certain. The trial was swift and decisive.

Frank and Joey would be hung by the neck until dead. As for Carson, well, thanks to the sheriff's testimony as to the fact that Carson was unaware of the presence of a firearm and the relationship between Carson and Sarah. He was sentenced to 10 years imprisonment without parole. The sheriff, with Carson, about to be transported by wagon to the prison outside of Denver says, "I'm sorry things went this way for you son. I know you didn't mean this to happen ,

I wish things were different for you." Carson says nothing. With that, the wagon left and Carson would spend the next 10 years in prison.

Now, Wichita had settled in his heart that his days of hunting down hardened out laws had come to an end. The life of a law man had left him as a lone rider, something that he was regretting. He had lost his family. He had lost a friend with the passing of the old prospector. He'd seen enough killing to last him a lifetime.

He also began to reflect on the fact that his obsession with hunting down outlaws had caused him to neglect someone else who needed his friendship a long time ago, that of a little boy back in Pagosa springs. So, Wichita begins to think to himself, maybe I'll head back and look up Carson and the Mills, see how the boy's doing, and then I'll decide. And so, he headed south all along the way, thinking about all the men that he had killed, some of which he could have brought in alive if in he'd a tried a little harder.

He also began to think about the fact that wherever he went, he was feared by the very folks that he was trying to protect. And in fact, in some cases, more than they feared the outlaws that he hunted. Well, the trail to the Mills farm gave Wichita plenty of time to think on all of this and more .

By the time he reached the Mills place, he had come to the decision that he would hang his guns and live a peaceful, quiet life from then on. That's what Annie would've wanted. Suddenly wolves howl all around, and spooked Wichita's horse .

"Whoa, there boy. Don't let them old wolves spook ya. Don't you worry. We'll be there pretty soon. I'm looking forward to seeing little Carson and Doc Mills and Sarah. It's been way too long. Besides, I think both of us could use a long rest and the Mills place is a good place for that.

Now, it was a warm summer day when Wichita arrived at the mills farm, he was looking forward to seeing old Doc and Sarah, but he was especially anxious to see Carson. Last time he'd seen him, he wasn't much more than baby, just four or five years old. He could remember Carson's smile and those big blue eyes that would look up at him.

He could only imagine what he would look like now. As Wichita approaches the cabin things seemed quite different. At first, it didn't cause any concern after all it had been 10 years since he'd seen the place. But then a man about 35 years old, much older than Carson, walks out of the barn and inquires.

"Can I help you?"

"Afternoon. I just stopped by to see the Mills family. I'm an old friend, hadn't seen him in quite a while."

"The Mills?" "Yes, sir."

"Well, they used to own this farm, but I bought it a few months back.

Come on in and rest yourself and we'll talk." "Thanks. Don't mind if I do."

Well, the man enters the cabin and he offers Wichita cup of coffee, or a drink a whiskey.

Wichita says "Coffee sounds good. Thanks a lot." "My name's Jacob. Jacob McClain. And yours?" "Wichita."

"Wichita. That's all?" "Just Wichita. That's all."

Well, Jacob pauses for just a moment. Pouring himself a cup of coffee as well. "Wichita, huh? Are you from down Durango Way?"

" Used to be."

"Well, I've heard of you. US Marshal, right? "No, not anymore. I gave that up."

"I see."

"You were gonna tell me about the Mills. What happened to them?"

Well, Jacob recalls how old Doc Mills had died of a fever more than two years ago, and how Sarah struggled, but she continued to raise Carson. He told of how despite Sarah's best effort, Carson had turned bad and in fact, he had taken part in a robbery that ended up with Sarah getting killed.

"I don't know much about the details. I came to the area after it all happened. Nobody wanted to buy the farm for a while. Everyone knowing the family so well and all, but I didn't know them, so I bought the farm and I got it at a really good price too. It's a really nice farm, and Sarah did a great job keeping the place up."

" Tell me what happened to the boy."

"Well, they say he was sent to prison somewhere around Denver. He had no hand in the actual killing, but he took part in the robbery. As for the other two? Well, they was hung by the neck till they was dead. That's all I know. Sorry, I can't be of more help Marshal."

"Wichita. Not Marshal, but thanks, Jacob. Thanks for the coffee and thanks for the info."

Well, they walked outside. Wichita looks around and says, "You're right. Sarah did a good job on this farm. It's a real nice place. This is a place my Annie would've liked." He then mounts up and he rides off.

CHAPTER 6

Telluride And The Final Test

Well with his bitterness and his anger laid to rest, and little hope of ever seeing Carson again. He decides to return to the only place that had brought him a real feeling of peace in years, the old prospects cabin just outside of Telluride. That was a place that he had returned to from time to time over the years, the only place that he could call home these days. There, he would live out the rest of his days in peace.

In time, Wichita would only become a legend and eventually the stories would be forgotten, and that's how it was. The stories, the fame, the legend, it was all but forgotten other names took its place in Colorado history. Names still famous to this day, names like Kid Curry, doc Holiday, Tom Horn, and the Sundance Kid.

Now, that was until the spring of 1910.

Now he had just returned from a hunt and shot himself a good size buck and he'd have plenty of venison for a while. He'd make jerky and clothes and hides and keep some meat packed in salt for later, but he was in need of some other supplies .

It was that time, once again, time to go to Telluride and resupply. That's something he had done once every few months or so for the past 10 years or more. When he would go to town he never spoke much to folks. He wasn't unfriendly, but he was just quiet. When he first started coming to town regular some would ask him his name but he would just smile and change the subject to the weather or something like that, or ask a question himself until folks got the idea and they just started calling him Old Timer.

Now, that was a name that he was comfortable with, a name that had fond memories attached to it. So, at first light, he gathered some gold dust and started down off the mountain heading to town.

Now, it was about noon when he reached the edge of town, and as he slowly rode in, folks would say "Howdy" and he'd smile and tip his hat, especially to the ladies. And he'd say howdy back.

From time to time he would stop in at one of the several saloons in town and have himself a drink, and today was one of those times.

"Howdy old timer, what do you have? The usual?"

"Yes sir. That would be fine."

"Been a spell since I seen you last. How are things up there in the hills?"

"Oh, they're fine. They're just fine ." Now sitting at the table at the other end of the saloon sat the local town Marshal and just about that time a deputy comes flying through the swinging doors of the saloon.

He's yelling "Marshal! Marshal! That young feller. He's at it again. He's over at the horseshoe, pushing folks around and looking for a fight. You best get over there before somebody gets hurt."

"Ah, I reckon I'd better."

Now the Horseshoe Saloon was just across the street and everybody in the place, with the exception of the old timer and the bartender, run over to the window to see what was gonna happen.

The old timer asked, "What's that all about?"

"Oh some young feller by the name of the Pagosa kid packing a pair of Colts, rode into town a few days ago and started bragging he was a gunfighter, saying he was taught by the fastest gun that ever lived. I don't know, some old time, US Marshal. He started pushing folks around.

Came in here last night and he'd a torn the place up, but the sheriff got the drop on him and stuck him in jail for the night. We's all hoping that he'd just cool off, and that'd be the end of it. I tell you that boy's a bad one and it sounds like he's at it again."

Well, someone at the window yells out, "Hey, look, the Marshal called him out."

"I wonder what's going to happen." "Here he comes."

So, the old man gets up from his stool and he joins the crowd to see what's happening. Well, there stood the Marshal, and about 30 feet in front of him was a tall, long haired man with steel blue eyes wearing two colts and ready for a fight.

The old man's heart began to race. He hadn't seen a gun fight in years, and what he was about to see brought back old memories, feelings that he thought he had forgotten years ago. What was worse was the fact that this young man who appeared to be in his late twenties looked exactly how he would've expected Carson to look.

The fact that he mentioned a US Marshal was something that the old timer just couldn't get out of his mind. "Could this be him?" He thought to himself.

Then they hear the town Marshal say, "Son, I told you last night to leave your guns in your room or leave town. I'm gonna take you in, keep you in jail for a while. Hand over them shooters."

Well, the young man just laughs and says, "you want my guns, Marshal then take 'em.

Without hesitation, the Marshal drops his hand to pull his colt. But with amazing speed, the young man pulls both shooters and fires two shots, hitting the Marshal in the shoulder, and right arm, dropping his pistol.

Now the deputy watching all this from somewhat of a distance, fires from the street and misses. The gunfighter returns fire hits the deputy high in the arm. "Anybody else ?anymore law in this town gonna take my guns?" Well, everyone in town, including the old timer, just quietly close their doors, pull their shades, and continue with their business, afraid to do, or say anything.

While the old timer sits back down on his chair with all kinds of thoughts racing through his mind and listening to the folks in the saloon. Someone says, "What are we going to do about that boy, who's gonna stop this Pagosa kid?" Another says, "Yeah, and the US Marshal, he's a week away. Even if we telegraph him right now, there's no telling what that young feller will do. He may kill somebody next."

The old timer still pondering the possibility that this young man could be the little boy he had found and developed such a fondness for years ago. He thinks to himself, "if that young man is who I think, this is my fault, I should have returned. I shouldn't have left him alone."

He pauses in thought for just a moment, and then he says out loud, "Wait a minute, it ain't none of my concern. I need to get back to the cabin and mind my own business. Besides, it can't be him." Well, one of the town folks in the saloon says to the other, "What's he talking about? Does that old man think he can do anything? He needs to just go back to the hills. He's just in the way." Just then something caught the old timer's ear. The bartender says, "They say that that boy just got outta prison down Denver way. They should have never let that one out. I'm telling you right now,"

"Down Denver way," the old timer thinks to himself, that's where the farmer said that they sent Carson. To a prison somewhere around Denver. With that, frustrated and confused, he walked out the door, headed to the general store.

He was just going to get his supplies and head back to the cabin, he wanted nothing to do with this.

But then as some would say, "AS FATE WOULD HAVE IT" he suddenly spots this young gun fighter backing outta the barbershop. At first, the old man's inclination was to call out to the young man calling by the name Carson, but then he noticed his hand around the throat of the barber.

The old man watched as he slapped the barber to the ground, and then suddenly a little boy, about eight or nine years old, comes running out of the barber shop, yelling, "Get your rotten hands off my pa." Then the gun fighter turns and he slaps the boy down into the street and then kicks him with his boot.

Instantly, thoughts of whether or not this was Carson just disappeared. The old timer's thoughts turned to his own son who was brutally murdered. Already struggling to hold back old feelings and now seeing a child the same age as his own son treated this way. It was more than he could stand. Falling back to old instincts, the old man goes for his gun, but there is no gun. Several people in the street see the old timer and one yells out. "Good, idea old man, but what are you gonna do?" Well, the gun fighter turns, hearing what was said, and he sees an old man and he laughs out loud and says, "So you're itching to draw on me? Are ya old man?"

The old man just bows his head down and he doesn't say nothing. The gun fighter laughs and then he continues. "Go home, old man but if'n you wanna play gun fighter, come back packin and we'll play."

Now, that night he got very little sleep, dreams haunted him all night. Dreams of Annie and Little Luke, the hold up in Durango and little Sally, he dreamed of the young brave that died in his arms. He dreamed of the cabin where he found Carson's family tortured and murdered. He dreamed of the old prospector whom he loved.

He saw every face of every one of the outlaws that he had killed, murderous low-down snakes, bent on killing and hurting anyone and everyone that got in their way. Every face he saw suddenly came together to form the face of this mysterious young gun fighter and that face formed into the face of Carson. A boy of five years old.

The old man realized that the fate of this young man and indeed his own for that matter, lay in his hands, in his gun hand to be exact.

If'n he didn't stop this young man, he would eventually kill someone if'n he hadn't already. And if he didn't find out who this Pegosa kid really was, why he would never have peace or rest ever again. In the old man's mind, if this was Carson, somehow it was his fault that the boy was here and it was up to him to stop him now.

Unable to sleep, the old timer rose up, pulled out an old chest from underneath the bed, and he pulled out a long barrel, 44 Colt, strapped on his holster, and he rode to town.

Now, it was well after midnight when he reached town. The sky was overcast and it was pitch black, not so much as a single beam from the moon . The Pegosa kid had been making his rounds going from one saloon to another, picking fights, bullying folks, knowing that no one in town had the courage to challenge him. As the young gunfighter walked by an alley, he heard the distinct sound of a pistol hammer being pulled back. Before he could react, he felt the cold barrel of a large caliber pistol suddenly pressed against the back of his neck.

"Put your hands up." A voice said from behind the Gunfighter, "You so much as twitch and I'll end it right here, right now. Drop that gun belt." Well, the kid reluctantly reaches down to unstrap his holster and says, "you too much of a coward to face me, man to man."

The gunman hits the kid on the ear with his pistol. "Ain't nobody afraid of you, boy," the Pegosa kid in pain yells, "what do you want from me?" "I want some answers."

"What kind of answers ? " to start with? Where are you from?" "Lots of places. What's it to you?"

"How'd you get that name? Pagosa Kid."

"None of your business. The gunman hits him again. " You want to try again."

Angry and in pain. The kid answers. " I grew up there when I was in prison. They just called me the kid from Pegosa. That name just stuck."

"What about your ma and pa? Are they alive?"

"What business is that of yours? What do you want from me?" The gunman then presses the barrel of his gun under the ear of the young gun fighter.

He presses hard. "I ain't asking you again, boy. Are your folks alive?"

The kid answers in a softer, calmer voice now with sadness, " No, my folks were killed when I was just a boy. I, I, I don't remember much about 'em "

"What's your real name?"

"My name? My name is Carson. Carson Mills."

The voice behind him says nothing but the barrel of the gun is no longer pressed hard against the ear, and the kid thinks to himself, that's strange. Who is this? Then the young gunfighter regains his hard attitude and says, "Listen, Mr. If you're planning to kill me, just get it over with. Otherwise, give me my guns and face me."

"I ain't going to kill you, at least not yet. But I got one more question and you best tell me the truth." Well, hoping for the right answer. "Have you ever killed anybody,"

"I'm gonna kill you. If I find out who you are, once again, he hits the kid in the ear, "I ask you question boy, I expect an answer."

"No, I, I ain't killed no one except" stopping and thinking of Sarah and still blaming himself for her death.

"Except who."

"Except for, I mean, I didn't kill her, but, but it was my fault."

The gunman lowers his pistol and he slips away into the cover of the night. The young gun fighter puzzled by what had just happened, but angry as well. Yells out. "I'll find you Mr. And when I do, you're dead. You hear me? You are dead ".

Later that morning, it was about 10:00 AM some of the town folks noticed the old timer at the edge of town just standing there with a gun strapped to his hip. It was a long barrel colt 44. The old man pulls the colt out of this holster and checks to make sure that he's fully loaded. Then, with incredible speed, he spins the gun in his hand, first forward, then backward and in one easy motion right back into the holster. Folks looking on were at a loss of words.

They never seen this quiet old timer from the hills handle a colt like that or at all for that matter. The look on his face was determined. He had the look of a man comfortable with a gun on his hip. He had the look of a gun fighter. Then, he calls out to the young boy standing next to the general store son.

"Do you know the Pagosa kid?" "Yes, sir. I know who he is."

"Go find him, son and tell him that I'm waiting for him. Tell him it's time to play. He'll know what it means."

The young boy starts looking for the gun fighter and then he finds him coming out of the Horseshoe Saloon. Terrified the brave young boy tells the gunfighter everything that the old timer had told him.

The Pagosa kid laughs out loud and says "That crazy old man, this should be fun." And he slowly walks to the edge of town. By this time, the whole town was aware of what was about to happen, and so everybody gathers around expecting that the old timer is about to be shot dead. As the gun fighter approached the old man, not taking his eyes off the kid for a second bends down and ties down his holster, and then he stands ready for the fight.

The gunfighter stops about oh, 40 feet from the old man, and then he says, "I see you're packing a pistol there. That's a pretty big gun for an old timer. It's a pretty old one too."

The kid says softly to himself. "I haven't seen anyone packing one of those since" Then dismissing that thought. The kid continues to speak out loud. "You sure it works?"

The old timer replies "This colt and me. We've grown old together, son, don't you worry as you're about to see it works just fine. I'm here to say one thing to you, boy, I've known men like you all my life, taking what they want when they want it and not care who they hurt along the way. And if that's the way it is with you, well your way ends right here, right now. Regardless. Your gun fighting days are over. Fill your hand" As quick as thought, with lightning speed, the Pagosa kid draws his colts, but before he could even level them to fire. The old man draws fires, and holsters his shooter in one easy motion, hitting the gun fighter in the right hand, knocking his gun several feet away.

With the kid still holding the second shooter and raising it to fire.

The old timer, draws again and fires , knocking the gun from his hand. The kid falling to his knees and holding his bloodied hand, yells , "Who are you? Old man?" The old timer answers, "I'm just a foolish old man son. Besides who I am, that ain't important, what's important is I know you, Carson Mills."

He then realizes that this is the man in the alley, in pain and in anger.

He screams out, "Who are you?"

The old timer pauses and then he says, "I'm the man that's gonna let you live, and I'm gonna let you live for one reason, because maybe, just maybe, there's a chance that somewhere inside you is the same decent kid that I knew years ago."

Carson Mills thinks silently to himself. "What is he talking about? He can't , He can't be."

Then the old man continues. "But if not, if this is the life that you wanna lead, then you go tell your friends and anyone else like you not to come to Telluride. Their kind ain't welcome here. You tell'em Wichita's in town." The Pagosa kid, wounded, humiliated, beaten, looks up with the slightest bit of a smile and a hint of pleasing relief.

And he simply says, "Marshal, it's, it's you." And with that, just like 20 years ago, the old timer extends his hand and the young man reaches out. A crowd gathers around, and Wichita helps Carson to his feet.

Well, folks, that's my story. Just as it happened. These are the things that I've seen and heard about my friend, Wichita.

As for me, I'm over 80 years old now, but you'll still find me sitting on the porch of the old jailhouse here in Durango, still wearing a deputy's badge for that matter. Folks around here just ain't got the heart to put me out to pasture, I reckon.

Things have changed around here though, since those days. Haven't seen or heard of a gunfighter like in the old days for years now. But still once in a while, some folks will come through and ask about those days. From time to time, Wichita's name will come up. One reporter from back east came through town once and ask if I knew what had happened to the killing Marshal of Durango. Wanted to know if he's still around and if Durango was still wild and untamed. I just told him, ain't too many bad men come around here anymore. Well, he asked "why." I simply said, "well, sir, bad men still fear the fast hand of the law, at least in these parts."

He then asked me, "how do you know that he's still around?"

That's when I told him "If 'n you pass through the Rockies, and there ain't a cloud in the sky, but you hear the sound of thunder in the distance. Then chances are son, Wichita's nearby.